The Impossible Resurrection of Grief

The Impossible Resurrection of Grief

Cover art & design by Rachel Lobbenberg
racheldesign.myportfolio.com

Edited by Selena Middleton

Published by Stelliform Press
Hamilton, Ontario, Canada
www.stelliform.press

Library and Archives Canada Cataloguing in Publication

Title: The impossible resurrection of grief / Octavia Cade.
Names: Cade, Octavia, 1977- author.
Identifiers: Canadiana (print) 20210096489 | Canadiana (ebook) 20210096519 | ISBN 9781777091767 (softcover) | ISBN 9781777091774 (ebook)
Classification: LCC PR9639.4 C33 2021 | DDC 823/.92—dc23

The Impossible Resurrection of Grief

Octavia Cade

Stelliform Press
Hamilton, Ontario

1

The Sea Witch lived in an abandoned saltwater pool. I knew her when she was called Marjorie and had the office next to mine at the university, but when the Grief came on her she stopped coming into work and set herself up at the derelict public pool with a stack of useless journal articles and a life-time supply of plastic. The only reason she let me in the door anymore was when I brought her more.

"I don't want this," she said, shoving plastic bowls back at me, plastic bottles, even a plastic hairbrush. She hesitated over cling-wrap. "I only want the bags," she said, but the cling-wrap disappeared into her pockets anyway.

The bags were getting harder to find. Not like the old days, when everything was packed into them at supermarkets. But plastic endures. It always had, and asking around netted me the odd stash shoved in the back of cupboards and forgotten.

"Marj," I started, but she hissed and flinched, hunched in on herself. "I'm sorry. Sea Witch, is there nothing else I can get you? Nothing else that you want?" We were friends, once. Still would be, if I had my way, but friendship is a mutual choice and the Sea Witch had forgotten mutuality. I'd brought her so many different objects but she rejected them all, discarded everything from a former life she didn't want to keep. I tried blankets, because it was cold at the pool with the roof fallen in and rubble scattered over the space below, but the Sea Witch shook her head and huddled into corners, out of the way of the worst of debris and indifferent to the cold night air and the rain that fell through the remnants of roof. I tried books, because there'd been a time when the Sea Witch had loved to read, and the journal articles she kept in small neat piles even now spoke of a fingertip hold left to literacy, but she never so much as glanced inside their covers. Even the collection of fairy tales she'd had since childhood, the Andersen which had once been her favourite, failed to move her. I left it anyway, balanced on the pool edge over the old intake pipe that had once filled the pool with ocean water. I'd tried food — which she didn't eat — and medicine — which she didn't take — and I'd dragged other people there, doctors and psychologists, every sort of therapist I could think of. They all shrugged and turned away, weariness etched into the small sloping shelves of shoulders. "She's a great deal better off than most of them," said one. "Even the plastic ... I suppose it's a sort of therapy. And I'm sorry, but we just don't have the beds."

I even brought her, once, the charred remnants of a ship's wheel, picked out of the fire she'd set that night on the beach. I thought it might remind her. She'd stared at it for a long time, looked through it as if into a past ocean, and turned away.

"Sea Witch," I said again. "Is there nothing I can do for you?"

She looked at me then, with empty eyes. "Can you bring it back?" she said.

It's the one question they all ask, and the answer is always the same.

We met on an overseas trip, Marjorie and I. Both of us were travelers, and we both preferred to travel alone and make friends as we went. Truthfully, I wasn't looking for a friend at the time — for the duration of the trip, I'd decided to consider them a distraction. I'd wanted to visit Palau for so long, to swim with the jellyfish for so long, that when I was finally able to go I wanted nothing to interfere with my focus. It was to be a concentrated experience, and one that might never come again.

Jellyfish Lake was a small saltwater lake clouded with migrating cnidarians. The golden jellyfish, isolated from the outside world, posed no danger to humans. Although they possessed the stinging organs of other jellies, theirs were so weak that people could swim through the soft, billowing clouds of them without fear. The jellyfish migrated through the lake during the day, and snorkelers could swim with them, with thousands of jellies, with millions of them, and see in their lovely, delicate forms the histories of another life. They pulsed around me like little golden hearts, shimmering in the surface layer of waters, and it was as close as I've ever come to religious communion. Insulated from the world above by water, it was as if the jellyfish and I were the only creatures alive that mattered, and their bells beat in time with my heart.

We weren't allowed to do anything more than snorkeling. The lake was layered, and below the oxygenation of the upper waters, the thin surface of visibility, was hydrogen sulphide, which was toxic when absorbed through the skin. Moreover, the bubbles from scuba diving might have damaged the jellyfish, which was a reason more important to me than perhaps it was to the other tourists — with the exception of Marjorie.

"Though it's funny," she said afterwards, making conversation as our hair dried in ropes around us. "That danger beneath, and the way we refuse to go there. To see for ourselves. It would be stupid, I know, but how good are we at ignoring something that's only a few metres away? Something close enough, almost, to reach out and touch?"

I paid small attention. Truthfully, I'd forgotten the toxic layer as soon as I saw the jellyfish around me, that enormous silent swarm. They were so beautiful, and so *present*, that anything that wasn't them had been wiped clean out of me. I couldn't think of anything else, and I didn't want to. All I wanted was to bask in the experience, and to remember how connected it had made me feel to them, as if my flesh had taken on aspects of jellyfish, free-floating and delicate and perfectly suited for the world in which they found themselves.

It was only later that I realized I'd bonded with more than jellyfish. When Marjorie rang to tell me her university had a position opening up that would suit me I didn't hesitate to apply. She'd become one of my closest friends, a bond begun in lake water and wonder, and when I started my first day on campus she left a stuffed jellyfish on my desk, holding in its tentacles an invitation to come sailing with her on the boat she had just bought.

"Do you think it will ever happen to us? The Grief, I mean."

I should have listened harder. Instead I put it down to a temporary melancholy, and a temporary recurrence of the realization of loneliness. Marjorie's relationship with her boyfriend had just ended, and I saw sometimes how she looked at George and me, the comfort we found in each other then. So I made her come out with me instead, left George at home with his easel, and took her dancing until our feet blistered and stabbed, and melancholy was forgotten amid pulsing beats and pretty drinks.

Grief was never something I was comfortable thinking about. I mean, no-one *enjoyed* navigating absence — the common experience of loss that came with funerals and memorial services and disappointments — yet I was as competent with these small sorrows as anyone else. But Grief, the undermining upwelling of loss in response to ecosystem devastation, the failure of conservation, was far harder to comprehend. I acknowledged it as little as possible. Still, it took real effort to look away from anything that had so much power, and so much spread. Like a contagion, it ran through entire families, through populations and with random outbreaks, until everyone knew someone who had it, who had succumbed.

"It's the experience of loss," the psychologists said, but more than that it was a loss underlined by guilt, because that loss had no natural cause; not if you didn't count humans as natural, and I didn't. We weren't thunderstorms, nor did we blunder about, blind as bacteria. We had the capacity for choice, and what we had chosen — what we continued to choose — was death.

The shift in climate that we'd ignored for so long, that we'd only given lip service to preventing ... when it came it took so many of us with it, took us with floods and droughts. That was a small thing, really, and we were practised at looking away, so long as it only happened to other people, in other places. But when it started taking what lived with us — the birds and beasts and creatures that we loved, the green world that grew up around us, well. That was a loss we hadn't prepared for, for all we had allowed it ... encouraged it, even, through our choices.

It had never occurred to me — to any of us — how intensely we could mourn another species once that species was gone.

It wasn't the same for everyone. Some people didn't get it at all. Some people got it more than others — there was a higher rate of Grief in Indigenous populations, another negative metric people didn't want to acknowledge lest it highlight their own culpability and continued privilege. Some people were set off by old extinctions, some by new. Some felt it well up inside them with each new charred koala, burnt to death by bushfires. For some it was the sight of starved rockhopper penguins, for some the quiet, empty spaces where the little rock wrens had been, or the fading of alpine buttercups. The skeletal bleaching of the Great Barrier Reef had triggered the Grief of entire communities, and looking back now, I realized that there Marjorie had shown her susceptibility.

"It's all right for you," she said. "No matter what happens, you'll always have your jellyfish."

I wish I'd seen less bitterness. I wish I'd found another way to share the jellyfish with her. A better way. But with the Reef gone, there was no substitute for her, nothing she could ever learn to love so well.

The thing about Grief: once it comes it never leaves. The Grief is spiralling down and down into loss that can never be recovered, that will never lack culpability. It's the guilt that makes it so devastating ... and so profoundly destructive.

The Grief always ends in suicide.

The day that Marjorie became the Sea Witch she fired her boat to ashes. The *Sea Witch* was too large, and too unwieldy, for her to haul it up into sands on her own, so she beached it at the highest point she could and waited for low tide. The sands around the keel were wet, and my footprints filled with water as soon as the weight was lifted, so I hoped for spluttering and a slow harmless guttering of flame, as all my efforts to talk her out of burning failed.

"I don't want her anymore," she said.

"Then sell her! Or give her away if you have to. Don't destroy just for the sake of it." Marjorie loved the *Sea Witch*, no matter how much she tried to persuade me that she no longer cared. It had been freedom for her, and accommodation, and salt movement. I'd spent more than my share of time aboard, watching the affection on her face as she smoothed down surfaces, painted varnish over old wood, talked to every sail and joint.

"Why not destroy for the sake of it?" she said. "Isn't that what we've always done?" That utterance was an exaggeration and a culmination both, because Marjorie had spent her life in conservation, and it had failed her as much as she had failed it. She'd tried, again and again, to bring back and build up, and the repudiation of that wasn't just false, it was wallowing.

"If you can't bear to watch, you can go home," she said, but I couldn't. That would be abandonment and we'd been friends so long. I wouldn't forgive myself. Already I could see the Grief rising in her, though I didn't want to. Once manifested it never left, only got worse and worse until the Grief was all that was left. The Grief, and the ways of ending it.

Part of me was afraid she'd throw herself into the fire, burn herself down alongside the *Sea Witch*. That was what made me stay; that was what made me hope for the futility of burning ... that perhaps she'd see the futility as well as the flames and snap herself out of it.

I should have expected accelerant. There was no hysterics, no determined rush to annihilation, just a quiet slopping of fuel that sounded like seashore, a match, and the end of the vessel. It burnt quickly enough and Marjorie stood back and watched with folded arms, never made so much as a move towards the conflagration once she'd sparked it.

"Is it enough?" I asked her, when the *Sea Witch* had burnt down to wet sand and ashes, mostly, with parts of her left over for wreckage. The wheel had kept its shape; I could see its print in the sand, half-buried. The Sea Witch's course was set.

"It's never enough," she said.

The *Sea Witch* skimmed over water, light and beautiful. I could feel the crash and drag of waves reverberating through her wood; it made the boat feel alive. In the sunlight she was warm wood over warm water, curves and salt spray and the sails pulled taut in wind.

"At least something here is alive," said Marjorie. It was hyperbole but not one I pointed out, because there was such dislocation in her eyes that to address it seemed cruel. It's hard to lose a life's work, and her research on the Reef had changed to something that no longer appealed — a necropsy in many parts. The species left behind were not ones she felt any sympathy for.

"You can see them down there, clinging," she said, of the starfish, the Crown of Thorns. Warming water and migration saw them overwhelm the fragile corals, and their sinuous, grasping arms caught at the coral and devoured it. "I hope they die when so much of their food has gone," she said. "I hope they *die*."

Her vehemence reassured me. Such loathing for another living creature had never, it seemed to me, been a hallmark of Grief. George pointed out after, as kindly as he could, that I had never been an expert on Grief, so how would I know? My specialty was jellyfish, and I'd refused to look at other layers, floated in the sunlit surfaces of my own intellectual waters, not even glancing down at the danger beneath. But I believed that she was safe, that hatred had been inoculation for her, and that her vocation and her emotion could transform a career in preservation to one in pest control. It seems so foolish now. If something had come to kill the jellyfish of the world — if it had left that little lake in Palau a sterile and barren place — I'd have wanted to murder too, but it would have done nothing for the miserable pain of absence.

"It reminds me of Andersen," she said, staring down into waters which were so full, once. "I named this boat for him, you know. The Sea Witch in "The Little Mermaid," she lived in an underwater forest. I think it was meant to be terrifying, full of tentacles and polyps and skeletal things, but all I saw when I read it was anemones and sea snakes and all the coral creatures. I know it said no flowers grew there but I always thought they did — that stupid mermaid never saw anything but what she wanted. Now I'm not so sure. The Sea Witch lived in a place of power, but all that's down there now is tentacles, like the story said, and they grab and grab until there's nothing left, until the wonder is all torn apart.

"I always felt," she said, "that I was never the one who'd look away. I wanted to be the Sea Witch, so clear-eyed. Now I wonder if the mermaid was all I ever was." She shook her head. "If there was ever a Sea Witch who lived down in the coral she's not there anymore."

"Maybe she took her power with her," I offered.

"I hope so," said Marjorie, her eyes on depths and horizons in turn. "I hope she found new places to make her bargains, when the old ones died around her."

In the saltwater pool, the Sea Witch was crafting. Plastic ran through her fingers like water, her long fingernails shredding the thin material into strips that matched the ragged bell-shaped curve of her skirt. If there'd been water in the pool, more than the puddles the ruined roof let in, it might have billowed around her as if she were a jellyfish, but there wasn't. Instead the plastic lay limp as the skirt, lacking the animation that would cause the thin strips of either material to float and shift in water, detritus that mimicked movement and found itself swallowed by unwitting gullets. Poor sustenance for the starving bodies of birds and fish and turtles, for under-nourished dolphins.

"Can you bring me those papers?" she said. Not looking at me, because she didn't anymore. All her attention was in her hands, their mechanistic motion of shred and twist and how the dry repetition of it flaked her flesh, drew blisters with the transparent surface of cling-film.

I'd thought the journals she kept were her own. That is, journals that had published one or another of her papers, useless as she now thought them to be, reflecting as they did an ecology that no longer existed. But when I picked among them, I saw a diversity greater than I'd expected, and research from fields not her own. Some were new. Some were decades old. Terrestrial biology, geography, urban planning. Most researchers, I knew from my own experience, rarely had time to read outside their own specialty. If there was a common thread I couldn't see it.

The Sea Witch was scrunching papers, crushing them in her fists to make them small, unreadable, the words blurring into each other. Wanting to help, to connect with the shell of someone I'd once known as well as myself, I tore a paper for her, made the page compact and wrinkled, handed it over.

"Not that one," she said, and how could she know, barely ever looking up as she did?

"One's much the same as the other, isn't it?" It was a flippant response. Deliberately so. There had to be some way to break through to her, to get her to talk about more than plastic, more than absence, the great sucking whirlpool that Grief had made of her mind. She talked so little now. Barely more than she looked, and that was not at all. I tore the next page slowly, loudly, trying to get her attention.

"Not that one either," she said, and sighed. "Don't you even see what it's about? Don't you even notice?"

I smoothed out the crumpled page and looked for keywords. "Something to do with transport stations and school districts. The effective placements of city planning, at a guess."

The Sea Witch didn't look at me, but her hands stilled in her lap. She sat there, silent as stone, until it became clear I didn't understand, and then she sighed again, a small, sad sound. "Table of contents," she said.

I flipped to the beginning of the journal, started reading titles aloud. When I read one that described future-proofing coastal infrastructure against climate, her hands began to move again. "That one," she said, and I could see her shoulders soften a little at the sound of tearing.

In summer, I persuaded Marjorie to take the *Sea Witch* out to marvel at the blooms of box jellyfish. They were far more attractive afloat than washed up on beaches. Even if I couldn't swim in every swarm — the stings were unpleasant and, in box species like *Chironex fleckeri*, could be fatal — I still found them a wonder, and reassuring. They were more tolerant of climate change than many organisms, able to adapt to warming waters and lower oxygen content, and if the once-warnings of jellyfish seas had not entirely eventuated, there were certainly more of them than before, and their populations were spreading.

Stretched flat on the deck with my head over the side, I stared down at the ocean, my arms crossed beneath my chin. It was an awkward position, but one that allowed me to get close enough for a good view of the jellies that floated below. Their bodies brushed against the side of the hull. They looked so delicate, and so innocent. "Not everything is gone," I said.

"They're a sign that a lot is, though," Marjorie replied — for her, the warmth that brought the jellies also brought the hungry, migrating starfish, and made the Reef a more vulnerable place. The increased presence of predators, combined with the slow bleaching of the coral due to rising temperatures, undermined the entire ecology.

"They're part of your Reef too," I said, but the look on her face told me that the Reef was more to her than the success of a single organism. It was an ecosystem, and one past balance or return. No wonder she didn't see the jellies as marvelous, a reminder of the wonder of our time at Jellyfish Lake. That experience was far behind her, the memory lost in the hazard of the present.

"Some of them can get bigger than humans," I reminded her. "Bells over two metres wide and tentacles over thirty metres long." It was the greatest day of my life, the day George and I saw a lion's mane swimming off the coast of New Zealand, on an early trip taken to visit his family. I've heard stories of similar-sized creatures in the waters of Japan, where I've never been — Nomura's jellyfish. It made me happy knowing they existed, still, that they were thriving in a world where so much no longer was.

The ones below us were considerably smaller. One of them looked strange, not like the others. I was close enough that I could reach down and snag it, but before my fingers touched the water Marjorie grabbed at my arm. "It'll sting you," she said, and it was true that swimming in this particular swarm would see me hospitalized or worse. Beaches were closed regularly over summer, when a swarm like this moved close to the coast.

"Not this one," I said, and what I brought up wasn't a jellyfish at all. It was a plastic bag, somehow twisted and swollen so that when floating it could pass for jelly.

"Horrible things," I said, scowling, and got up to stuff the bag somewhere safe, until we could get back to shore and dispose of it properly.

"Yes," said Marjorie, absently, still staring down. "Horrible."

I'd never swum in the saltwater pool. For me, it had always been a wreck that kids sneaked into at night on dares. The pipes that used to fill it, that came from the ocean, were capped. It seemed a difficult task, in retrospect — having to filter all the things that could have come in. Those filters were long since gone. Perhaps they were looted, perhaps recycled, but if the pipes were opened back up now, salt water would fill the pool and with it would come the jellyfish. Not the golden jellyfish of Palau either, but the ones with powerful stings. Ocean swimming was more hazardous now, though for people like me it was perhaps more beautiful. So much of the danger came from migrating jellies, but the sea had always been a dangerous place. Tides could kill as quick as toxins, and no one who had seen tentacles drift for metres in the currents could ever forget the multiplicity of threat, no matter how much buoyancy was gifted to them by saltwater.

The Sea Witch, in her empty pool, created jellyfish of her own. She made them out of plastic bags, forming pieces of floating trash into the mimicry of movement. If I'd known this was what she wanted them for I'd never have brought the bags to her. I didn't care how limp they were, stranded on the dry bottom of the pool. No one made something like this without expecting them — without *wanting* them — to float.

"You *know* what plastic does!" I told her. "You *know* how dangerous it is to sea life." The remnants of populations that would get caught in it, that would swallow it and starve.

The Sea Witch shrugged. "So?" she said. "We kill everything anyway. It's what we do." The Grief was speaking through her, but I'd never heard of it manifesting as an active agent of further destruction. She held out a plastic jelly she'd finished wrenching into shape. "Look," she said.

Inside the bell was paper. A page, well insulated, and ripping through the plastic I found old warnings. Of what would happen if we didn't change, of what would happen if we didn't stop it, the shifting consequences of climate. I knew these papers. I'd written some of them myself. None of them were ever listened to. Certainly few of the recommendations were ever followed.

"Nothing we said made a difference. We might as well have said nothing at all," said the Sea Witch, disconsolate, a plastic comb in her hands. She turned it over and over. I remembered her refusing a hairbrush when I brought it to her, though it had been plastic as well. The comb hadn't been used on her hair. Even from a distance I could see the handle had been sharpened into a blade. "We might as well have been voiceless," she said. "We might as well have given up our tongues." And then she cut hers out, swiftly, brutally, with the comb edge of sharpened plastic, the comb I never knew she had, and her blood and my vomit spattered over the pool floor.

The Sea Witch, red-chinned, red-throated, recovered before I did. By the time I looked up from bile she had opened the pipe that connected the pool to the ocean. Saltwater streamed in, and brought the ocean with it. With the filters long gone, the currents brought fragments of kelp and floating algae. I saw a small fish sucked through, an ice-cream wrapper, a crab. A beer can. And between them all the jellyfish: the real, and the imagined.

At first I couldn't tell them apart. The Sea Witch hated jellyfish, but her mimicries moved as if they were flesh not flotsam. The plastic jellies rose with the waters, and the papers within their silent bells were accusation and consequence, the cost of looking away. The real jellyfish, the ones sucked in from the outside, swarmed between them, their tentacles caught in eddies and plastic. There were so many of them. I managed to get myself to the edge of the pool and out, but the Sea Witch was weakened by Grief and blood loss, and she was not fast enough. The jellyfish wrapped her in their gossamer tentacles, a beautiful angry bloom, and kept her there until her screams and Grief were silent.

2

The package arrived three days after a memorial service that
hardly anyone attended. I didn't know what I expected — part
of me, feeling the shape and heft of it, hoped for a book of fairy
tales. The Andersen, which was by now sodden and disinte-
grating at the bottom of the pool, would have been a touching
present, one left behind by a woman who could no longer bear
what she had made of the world.

Instead, it was letters. A packet of them, tied together, all
from the Sea Witch, and all to someone I didn't know. I tried to
read them, but they were misery and running ink, the decom-
pensation of a once-brilliant mind into madness. There was no
apology, no explanation. Many of the pages made no sense.
The writing was more scrawl than recognizable letters, and the
lines crossed each other in different directions, as if the writer
overlaid new understandings on top of old, and couldn't see
that the earliest expressions of comprehension obscured the
later. The notation at the top of one of them, made in a different hand and with precision in the ink, was equally unclear.
"The sanest of them all," it said. The writing was the same as
that on the front of the package, the same as that on the return
address.

"If this is an invitation," said George, "I suggest you don't
accept." We were divorcing, the dissolution of our marriage
regretted on both our parts. He wanted children, and I didn't.
The change of heart was mine. He pored over the
letters with all the attention he gave to the divorce agree-
ment — an attention born of scrupulous fairness and careful

consideration. He peered at me through glasses. "We both know it's an invitation."

"There's nothing that says I have to accept."

"Good. Don't. You've always been able to turn away, and I've always liked that about you." That he could say this even when he was one of the things I'd turned away from was almost enough to make me reconsider leaving him. If I'd cared for him less I would have stayed, but he'd been my best friend for over ten years, and I couldn't bring myself to compromise his happiness by insisting on a sterility that suited only one of us. "For all we know it was getting involved with people like this that made Marjorie turn out the way that she did." He waved one of the pages at me. "The sanest of them all, really? If someone sent me a letter like this I wouldn't be trying to justify it. I'd think they needed psychiatric help."

George had never called Marjorie the Sea Witch. Had flatly refused to do so, considered it catering to delusion where I called it a last kindness to a friend sinking into a darkness no one would ever be able to retrieve her from.

"I think she was more susceptible than I am." Less settled in the common world. "Come on, George. We both know I'm not the flighty type."

"It's never been flightiness that opens people up to Grief," he said. "You know that as well as I do." He stacked the letters neatly, almost fussy in his movements — a precision I'd always found slightly incongruous when contrasted with the sheer size of him, and the thick strong fingers that made mine look pale and flexible as tentacles.

"It's never been curiosity either," I said, but that was belief on my part, not established fact.

Truth was no one knows what prompted a person to turn to Grief. Some said it ran in families. Others that it came down to vocation or brain chemistry. If there was a shared characteristic there might be hope for inoculation, but there was no vaccine, nor any psychological panacea that had proven effective. It was just waiting, until the day Grief hamstrung from behind and another person started to gnaw on themselves for the things they had or hadn't done, for the loss they couldn't recreate.

Marjorie's transformation into the Sea Witch had made Grief a frequent topic of conversation in our house. I still remembered the both of us in bed, the sheet pulled over our heads, lying on our sides and George's warm breath in my face. "Do you ever think it will happen to us?" I'd asked. "I don't think I could bear it."

"You'd only have to bear it if it happened to me," George replied, prosaic to the last. That was typical of him — his idea of comfort was a considered assessment of possibility. "If Grief came for you, you wouldn't care. You'd be too deep in it to mind."

His ability to reason both side of things wouldn't save him from Grief, but it made me feel better regardless, as if such careful fairness would act as inoculation. Truthfully, I was more concerned about myself. There, George was less comforting.

"I worry how easily you shut things out," he said. "It doesn't seem such a short step, sometimes."

That was a conversational path I hadn't wanted to go down. It was too reminiscent of our discussions about children.

I'd wondered if it were passivity that brought it on. George had only scoffed. "It's not passivity you're thinking of. It's accepting the inevitable and not liking it. This business with Marjorie is the first time you've really had to do that."

He didn't say "Nice for some," but I could see that he was thinking it. At first I thought he was talking about us, the divorce looming ever clearer on the horizon, but pressed warm against each other under the covers we had both wanted to pretend that our marriage was solid. "Tell me," I said.

"Hurt's easy enough to live with," he said. "If there's an end to it. Break your arm and it hurts, but it heals soon enough and the hurt goes away. Even a small pain, if it never leaves ... It wears you down," he said. "In the end it isn't the hurt that gets you, it's the *exhaustion.*"

Indigenous peoples suffered more from Grief, he said. The experience of watching the world change around them, the loss of land, was an old wound kept open.

"Do you hurt that way?" I asked, because even if I could no longer see myself staying with him he was my best friend still. The thought of his hurt was painful to me. It was also something I failed to understand. I was afraid if I couldn't understand it, one day I'd use that lack of comprehension to discount experiences that weren't mine. It wasn't a part of myself that I liked, that temptation to discard, but when George said I found it easy to limit myself he was telling an unpleasant truth.

"You're asking because I left." It wasn't a question, and George — who knew my small selfish spaces as well as anyone alive — regarded me with an honesty that silently spoke of the uneasy places he knew existed within himself. It was something I'd teased him about before, when the conversations between us were less fraught. So many New Zealanders had come to live in Australia, and many of those, like George, were Indigenous. The Grief had cut swathes through the people of Aotearoa, as it had with many communities, and Māori, like the other Indigenous populations, were over-represented. "Some lands are easier to love at a distance."

The last two times I'd suggested we travel back to see his family he'd refused. Not for reasons of dislocation or alienation. At least, that was what he said, and George was never one for prevarication or self-deception.

"I've lived here twenty years," he said. "This is home now."

I didn't ask if his new home was less exhausting. If he found it so, it had always been to my benefit. And maybe to his.

We learn to protect ourselves in the ugliest of ways.

Perhaps I should have asked, but sorrow is so terrifying.

George was right when he said the letters were an invitation. By themselves, I might have been able to leave well enough alone, but there was that little note scrawled across the top. *The sanest of them all.* There was nothing of sanity in the Sea Witch at the end. It had drained away, as it did with all the others like her. *The sanest of them all* could only have come from someone who was compromised themselves; someone who couldn't recognize lunacy and how it could pull a person down and into dark water. To expect answers from someone caught in the currents of their own Grief was madness.

Of course I went anyway. How could I not? George scowled and disapproved, but friendship has a claim even when the friend is gone. Those letters were sent to me for a purpose, and I intended to find out what it was.

The Sea Witch had sent her letters to an address in Tasmania, an island I'd never visited. That same address was on the back of the packet which passed those letters on to me. Travel was easy to book, and leave easier to obtain. The desire to travel showed an interest in life, something different from the obsession of Grief, and the university encouraged it.

"I don't care what the university thinks," said George. "There's something wrong here." He didn't ask me not to go, because it wasn't his place anymore and we were too careful in our boundaries now. But he drove me to the airport and slipped a packet of soft licorice into my purse and stood with his arms crossed while I checked in. *You've always been able to turn away, and I've always liked that about you,* he'd said, the man who had learned to turn away from home and family himself, and that was what I'd always liked best about *him*: his capacity to let go, easily and without apparent resentment.

"Just be careful," he said, and did not kiss me goodbye. "Call me when you get there."

I did call. I could give him that, at least.

Tasmania was green and blue and salt-scented, with wind so strong I had to braid my hair to keep it from tangling. It was cooler than the north, and as I headed towards the more mountainous centre I admired the deciduous beech trees and the rainforest. More than this, I admired the eucalypt forests, the tall enormous stands of swamp gum, breathing in their kerosene scents as I stopped underneath them for lunch, leaned against the crumbling bark of their trunks, and examined the hard little gum nuts that fell about me. They were so tight and contained and separate that I wondered how they ever survived.

I would have been more interested in sharing my impressions of it with George if I'd felt less disturbed. That wasn't an admission that would have made either of us feel any better about my being here, so I kept it to myself and walked into a place of extinction. In all that green and blue and salt, extinction was a familiar odour.

At my destination — the remote, run-down farmhouse that corresponded to the address on the packet of letters — photographs of the same striped animals adorned the walls like family portraits. Amid the still pictures, short videos played on wall-mounted screens. The recordings, like the photos, were taken as the species was dying. We had so little surveillance of them, and most of that was centered around extinction. On each screen, thylacines paced up and down cages, the last specimens of a lost bloodline. They were meaty, elongated creatures, with short legs and jaws that gaped like a basking shark's. They did not move like jellyfish, and I did not love them for it.

The woman who had welcomed me inside was old enough to be my grandmother, or Marjorie's grandmother. I wondered if that was why the Sea Witch had sent her so many letters. Marjorie's Gran had died when she was a child, and she had missed the relationship. Perhaps the Sea Witch found an old woman easier to confide in. So, following what I imagined was her lead, I called the old woman Granny. Not to her face. Her real name came with academic affiliation, with professorships and PhDs, but thinking of her as Granny reminded me that those impressive credentials belonged to the woman she had been before Grief struck her. Forgetting that Grief would have changed her — as Marjorie had changed into the Sea Witch — was a dangerous endeavour. Granny hid the madness well. That she still had an emeritus position was testament to her faculties. Looking for insanity as I was, however, I could see it seeping through to the surface from somewhere deep within her. There was the same mix of scatter and focus that I'd once seen in the Sea Witch, and for a brief moment I thought I saw Marjorie's eyes staring out of Granny's face.

"These are yours," I told her, handing her the packet of letters. I didn't need or want them. They were unpleasant reminders of what Grief did to my friend's mind. "How did you know to send them to me?"

Granny smiled, and it showed all her teeth. "We talked about you. Does that surprise you?"

"Yes. I'm not that interesting."

"You're unlucky," said Granny. "That *is* interesting. But there are so many unlucky people now. Still, you needn't worry. It's possible your fortunes could change."

"Unlucky?"

"Grief hasn't come for you yet. That's unlucky."

As if the avoidance of Grief was a misfortune she hoped would be remedied. "I'm happy the way I am. Don't mistake loyalty and curiosity for a tendency to melancholy."

"You're so certain you won't develop it, are you? Goodness. How extraordinary, to have the walking avatar of immunity here in my house."

That was a bold claim, and not one I was prepared to make. I wasn't superstitious and never had been, but to state that I'd never succumb to Grief was arrogant to the point of foolishness. "The universe dislikes hubris, I think."

"And yet here you are." Granny had a point, and George would have agreed with her. It was why the people who came down with Grief were shut away in hospitals, and why no one went to their funerals. Too much attention to the misery of others was a dark path in a dark wood, and such paths were easy to lose. It's why I approached Granny at her home, rather than her work. There were fewer eyes here, and fewer suspicions. I had a sufficiency of those already.

She poured me tea. Her forearms were skinny under three-quarter length sleeves, and as she held the pot over our cups, I tried not to look at the scars that marked them. Puncture marks and ragged slashes, they were livid and in various stages of healing. One wound looked as if it had barely stopped seeping, but Granny didn't mention them so I didn't either. Part of that was politeness, part of it was disturbance, and part of it was that I felt she was showing them off and I didn't want to indulge her. Instead, I sipped the tea that was too weak and too lemony.

She smirked at me over the edge of her teacup, and I suspected that my refusal to look was indulgence enough.

"You disagree with what she did," said Granny. "The Sea Witch."

"It's not a matter of disagreement," I said. "I understand there was no help for it. Marjorie wasn't well. She wasn't thinking clearly."

"You're calling her Marjorie out of spite," said Granny. "You never called her that while she was alive. You were too *kind* for that. I'm glad you don't feel the need to display that kindness any longer." She placed her teacup back on the saucer with a brittle *clink*. "Good. I was hoping you weren't a milksop."

I drank more of the revolting tea, if only to have an excuse not to answer. I didn't consider myself a pushover, but it didn't seem wise to admit it. Bragging of that sort encouraged people to experiment with how much pushing a person could withstand. Besides, that limited praise had given me an inkling as to Granny's reason for speaking to me in the first place.

"This is a recruiting pitch." Of all the ridiculous things — I could see George's face, the disgust and the skepticism. No one needed to be recruited for anything connected with Grief. It came or it didn't, and working with it too closely, looking at it too closely ... there were some who considered that invitation. "I already have a job."

Granny shrugged and poured herself more tea. The scars stretched like thick red webbing over her arm as she placed the teapot once more between us.

"You've kept your joy in the world," said Granny, stirring the sugar into her cup. "Those revolting jellyfish. I suppose someone has to love them."

There was no response I could give to that either. Climate has done for some species, and done better for others. I wished there was a correspondence to Grief but there wasn't. The man who gave the keynote address at a conference I attended two years ago was as involved in jellyfish as I am — his papers were required reading — but that didn't stop his Grief, and he'd hung himself five months after the symptoms first appeared, tears streaming from his eyes and as far from ocean as he could get, or so his mourning husband had claimed in the obituary. Whatever the dead man had Grieved for, it hadn't been jellyfish. The loss was something that no saltwater could soften.

Granny leaned forward. "How much could you love if the world were different?" she said. "Can you take that level of joy in something other than jellyfish?"

"I don't see why not." It was a flippant response, though, so I stopped to consider. "It's difficult to say. The world *isn't* different. If the jellyfish were all destroyed, the oceans would be an emptier place. They'd be a shadow of a marvel for me, I think. It would feel as if something had gone out of my heart. I'd hope I could find something to replace it, but who knows. It doesn't seem to work that way for others."

"The Sea Witch thought it might work that way for you," said Granny. "She said you had a facility for replacement."

"Doesn't sound very complimentary, that."

"I didn't say it meant to be. Truthful, though. Her perceptions were very much unclouded. She had a gift, you see. The sanest of them all. She could see what was needed. She could see she didn't have it. I think she was sorriest for that in the end ... That her Grief was so purely internal. Rubbish and plastic, the ghosts of organisms that hadn't died. She'd have been better focusing on the really dead."

As far as I was concerned, the Sea Witch focused on nothing *but* the dead, on an ecosystem that could never recover. The last thing it made her was better off. The loss of the Reef was sickening, and I'd vomited up that anger and depression, and perhaps that purging had kept me from a greater sense of loss, and one more ultimately futile. Acknowledgement of the dead was never the problem.

Granny stirred more sugar into her tea, and the spoon squealed along the side of her china cup. "What if she could have brought it back?" she said.

The kittens, the pups ... I didn't know what to call them.

"Joeys," said Granny, but the word didn't make a differ-ence. There were still ghosts in my lap. Small, nuzzling ghosts. I could see the faint pattern of stripes that started behind their shoulders and followed the spine over their rumps, the tail that seemed too long for their bodies, the round-eared, triangular face that reminded me of weasels. Miniature versions of the creatures that adorned Granny's walls in photograph and video.

"I didn't realize you'd been successful." This should have been all over the news — the resurrection of an extinct species. I'd been focused elsewhere, but how had I missed this?

"No one does," said Granny. "Let's just say this is a private project. And it's going to stay that way. We've spent many years trying to bring back the thylacines," said Granny. "Piecing together the DNA, failing again and again."

I didn't know why she felt my silence was guaranteed, but it was clear that she did, and that sent stillness down my spine like a harbinger. Stupid, stupid. I should never have forgotten that Grief is an insanity of spirit, brought on by loss and end-ing always in death. As far as I knew — as far as anyone knew — that death had always been suicide. Suicide in the wake of irredeemable loss, when there was nothing left to protect.

In my lap, little teeth were closing on my fingers, with nips as sharp as a puppy's.

"They didn't love thylacines like I do," said Granny, of her former colleagues. "I couldn't trust them. How could I trust anyone who hadn't known Grief to keep my darlings alive again?" There was an accident in the lab, she told me. One that she carefully orchestrated, and the project was so compro-mised by the loss that the laboratory closed down, the project in abeyance, and Granny was able to steal enough of their resources to carry on in secret. It was the focus and obsession of Grief, and by it these creatures were brought back from the brink, hidden away in an old house in an isolated area.

Coddled by a woman who conversed with suicides, and who saw sanity in the actions of self-murder.

"They sleep in my bed," she said. "Wrapped up in my jumpers. They know my scent, see." One arm reached out to stroke the small heads, bone-hard beneath fur. Her scars shone white in sunlight. They were astonishingly varied — thick, thin, puncture marks and dragging, the long razor cut on the once-tender skin on the underside of her forearm, following the vein. Granny marked where my eyes were and smiled. "I didn't cut deep enough," she said, and the tone was all wrong, a parody of confidence.

"You're affording me a great deal of trust," I said, and two cups of that terrible tea had done nothing for the sudden dryness in my throat.

"I'm showing you very little," snapped Granny, and her hand hardened in my lap, closed tight about a small, protesting body. The squeak it made recalled her to herself, and she snatched the beast into the folds of her own body, cuddling it and crooning apology. She glared at me over the small head, eyed the remaining creature in my lap distrustfully. "You made me hurt it," she said. "You hurt it."

"It was an accident," I said. "I'm so sorry." The Sea Witch had always told me, mournful, that my strength was in adaptation. It was foolish to find yourself swimming in dangerous waters and fighting currents. It was best to go with them, to cut across when you can't go against. I took the small, warm creature in my hands and held it out. "Perhaps you had better take him. I wouldn't want to harm him by accident. He is too precious."

"He *is* precious," said Granny, suspicious. Then the suspicion slipped from her face, and the change was so immediate and absolute that it could have come from nothing but Grief. "They sleep in my bed," she said. "Did I tell you?"

The thylacines had once been known as Tasmanian tigers. "They're not tigers," Granny said. "Don't look at the stripes. Look at how they *behave.*"

They joeys squirmed on Granny's lap, trying to get free. One tumbled to the floor and shook itself, before hopping on its two back legs to her ankles. The joey buried its teeth in the already ragged hem of Granny's trousers, easily shredding the material. The other crawled to the edge of her lap and stared down at its littermate, intent on the shredding and entirely indifferent to the pats that Granny bestowed upon it.

"Marsupial wolves," said Granny. "That was their other name: the Tasmanian wolf. Of course they're not really wolves either." Her face was as watchful as a hunter, the face of a woman who reveled in the bite. Her upper lip twitched, exposing glimpses of yellowed teeth. I couldn't tell if she were doing it deliberately, trying to unsettle me, or if it was an unconscious gesture, born out of intimidation and threat. I might have been invited, albeit implicitly, but my presence was still an intrusion, and the Grief that so unbalanced her was not trusting of outsiders.

"It was us that killed them," she said. "Changing climate made them vulnerable, and we did the rest. Hunting and hunting and hunting ... Their extinction was deliberate. We weren't so damn indifferent to them that we let the world take them. I suppose that's something to be grateful for, that we at least cared enough to do it ourselves. We liked doing it."

She blinked at me, slowly. "Do you like it? Hunting?"

"I've never tried."

"I think you'd be good at it. You can care for something and watch it die and *let* it die. I know all about you," she said, and what the Sea Witch hadn't told her she must have inferred somehow.

The truth was I *did* let the Sea Witch die. Or at the very least I didn't try hard enough to save her, and it wasn't a good death. Truth is even if I could have saved her, I don't know if I would have. She would only have tried again. And again, and again. The next time might even have been worse, more painful. That's what Grief is, I think: an unshrinking look at the inevitable.

Granny invited me to stay the night. I would have rather declined her offer, but I had yet to understand what she wanted of me, and I wasn't sure she would have let me go when that understanding was absent. She was old, of course, and most likely frailer than she appeared. I could have pushed past her if I wanted to. I could go to all the newspapers in the land if I wanted to. It would be the story of the century. But Granny was here, and those delicate creatures were here. They were sleeping in the bed with Grief, and all that talk of letting loved ones die made me worry for their safety.

I wished I could trust her as a caretaker, but I didn't, not entirely. I wished I could talk to George, but he wasn't answering his phone and such conversation as I could have made would only have disturbed him.

I decided to stay, and not to sleep. I sat up in a cold night in a cold bed, reading of tigers and wolves and marsupial beasts, their skeletons and observed behaviour. Granny had left a stack of journal articles by the bed, dissections of what their authors believed was a dead species. I wondered if the articles were a deliberate reminder of shredded paper and plastic bells, the fishing trail of a tentacle dragged through water, but how could she have known so much of what the Sea Witch had done? Perhaps their letters shared more than I knew; I had no way of knowing if I'd read them all.

Granny didn't sleep either. I could hear her up and down the hall all night, the quick pattering footsteps of the old when they are trying to be light and cunning creatures.

In the middle of that cold night, I ventured out into the hallway to search for another blanket, and realized what those footsteps really were. *Patter patter patter*, and it was only because the floors were hardwood that I could hear them. On another surface, nocturnal hunters would be so very silent ... Catching the dark outlines of shapes in the hall, my back slammed against a wall before my brain understood why. Fragments of my earlier reading surfaced between ragged breaths: a paper on thylacine physiology, and what their skeleton implied about their hunting techniques. All I could think of was the morphology of their limbs, the construction of elbow joints that suggested that thylacines were ambush predators, tigers rather than wolves. The two I'd held in my lap were too small for predation, but moonlight shining through windows reflected eyes a lot further from the ground than a tiny joey could account for. I could hear breathing over the footsteps, an almost silent panting, and I couldn't tell which breaths were mine and which were theirs, but there was a faint stench of feeding, as if meat had been left out for pets and the scent of it had stained their teeth and tongues.

The whole house was shifting with them, stripes and small sounds and that warm, meat-scented breath: the convergence of the dead and the living, and I didn't know if they hunted in a pack like wolves, or if together they were enough to bring down an animal so much bigger than they were. They were living in a house, but that didn't mean domestication — they weren't dogs, and if resurrection and care had changed their nature, I had no indication of it. They may have started out sleeping in Granny's bed, but the scars on her arms ... They were too big and too deep to have come from the joeys. Those marks had come from creatures that hunted. Creatures raised by a woman who had teased me with the prospect of hunting, and who I suspected enjoyed hunting herself. Both the stalking and the bloody death.

Can you watch something die and let it die? she'd asked, and whether she was speaking to me or of me I was no longer sure, but I locked myself in the bedroom, door shut against resurrection and marvel. Thylacines were nocturnal, with night vision much better than mine, and to attempt escape in darkness was a foolish endeavor. Better to wait until dawn, when they were asleep, I hoped, and I could make my way out of a window and run for the rental car. Yet when dawn arrived, I found all the tires on the car had been cut, leaving me stranded amid the eucalypts. There I would have stayed — for what, I don't know — except a car pulled into the driveway and the passenger door opened up, the engine still running.

"Get in the fucking car, Ruby," said George.

3

Turned out George hadn't answered his phone because he was in the air at the time. "You've still got location tracking on your phone," he said. "And I didn't ... I just felt there was something very wrong about all this."

He'd never been the superstitious type; had never dreamed a death only to be woken by a phone call announcing the same. "The worst that could happen is that I'd look like a bloody fool," he said. "Wouldn't be the first time."

Fool or not — and he wasn't, and had never been — I was never so glad to see anyone in my life. "You would not *believe* the time I've had," I told him, and explained everything, in hysterical, overwrought detail, after we'd traveled far enough that panic had calmed enough for complete sentences. I made him stop for breakfast in case disbelief at my story caused him to drive us into a ditch.

Halfway through my explanation, tucked into a quiet corner booth in a cafe, something stilled in him. A bitter, sardonic smile and then nothing. "What?" I asked when I was done and his face hadn't changed through my recount of resurrection.

"This place," he said.

I didn't understand, and he waved his hand at the window, a vague gesture to the land. "Tasmanian tigers weren't the only living things that went extinct here," he said. "There's a long history of hunting on this island."

Something I'd known about and forgotten, a horror not close enough to immediately recall. Conflict between the

33

Indigenous people of Tasmania and the colonial settlers resulted in slaughter and extermination orders, martial law and a white governor's instruction to shoot Indigenous inhabitants on sight. The mustering of the Black Line, where every able-bodied male settler was ordered to take part in an organized drive to sweep the island of its original inhabitants, in order to exterminate a people and their culture. How those settlers had stalked and trapped and murdered, how they'd hunted until all the faces left were white, and the meagre remnant of Tasmania's first peoples to survive the genocide had been dumped on a smaller, less hospitable island, to die of isolation and influenza.

Genocide and absence, and for some things, for some people, a corresponding Grief that never came. I'd seen an old woman in an old house, the descendant perhaps of a man who'd gone mustering on the Black Line, driven to insanity by the loss of a marsupial wolf but not the indifferent slaughter of a people. Had the destruction of Tasmania's first peoples ever induced someone like Granny — someone like me — to Grief, or was it only the absence of those so little like us that was memorialized in this way? I'd never thought to check, though the over-representation of Indigenous populations in suicide statistics was a grim, provoking question.

Of all the places to which George and I had gone on holiday over the years, we'd never come here. I'd suggested it, idly but more than once. George had never wanted to visit. He claimed it was because it made him think too much of home, and I'd always thought he was referring to geography and landscape instead of blood and conflict.

Hunting and hunting and hunting ... I suppose that's something to be grateful for. That their extinction was deliberate. We weren't so indifferent to them that we let the world take them. We did it ourselves. We liked doing it.

It was nothing to be grateful for.

"What am I supposed to do now?" I said finally, on my third cup of coffee and jittery with it, skimming over a sorrow that had never been recognized enough, at least not by me, the woman who had brought plastic to a friend who mourned more for coral than for culture. George let me do it, too, as if practice had taken away his resentment. I didn't ask if that were possible. I was more concerned with other possibilities. Such luxuries the lopsidedness of Grief had left us. The eggs I hadn't been able to finish sat uneasily in my stomach.

"Am I supposed to walk into a police station and say 'Hey, there's an old woman who's brought back marsupial predators from the dead, and I think she wanted me to help them hunt. You know, for food. Or she was planning to feed me to them herself. I'm not sure.'"

"They'd lock you up," said George. "Just long enough to call a doctor." He didn't need to say more. Irrationality, a sustained focus on an old extinction ... they'd call it Grief, and anything I said after that would be at first suspicious and then irrelevant. I'd likely get the same reaction from everyone — from Granny's colleagues, and from the press.

"It's a miracle you believe me," I said, hunting for strawberry jam in the little jars they brought with the toast. I wasn't hungry, but if I didn't do something with my hands I'd be clutching at my cup with a grip so tightly unsteady it would have spilled the coffee.

"Yes," said George, definitive. He'd never been much of a liar. I'd always found that inability to prevaricate an irritating trait. Now it was actually comforting, because if George thought — if he even suspected — that I'd fallen to Grief, he would have flat-out said so to my face.

"Well, you're not exactly fanciful, are you?" he said, shifting the coffeepot out of reach as I stretched to refill my cup. I shook my head, cheeks bulging with toast and strawberry. "Question is, what are we going to do now?"

It was the "we" that did it. Our marriage was ending, an ongoing process neither of us would stop, but when push came to shove it was still "we," an automatic standing-beside that not even divorce could shift. I burst into tears over the remains of a plate of scrambled eggs, hands over my mouth to prevent jam-coated crumbs from leaking out. George, faintly appalled at all the mess, fished paper napkins out of the dispenser and started mopping me up regardless.

We were on a flight to New Zealand the next day. I should have felt bad about all this flying — it was only making matters worse, with climate the way it was — but since I'd held in my lap a species brought back from the dead, everything else seemed a little ... distant was the best word for it. Like the world had been set slightly askew, and gravity had become less than it was.

I called the police while George was organizing tickets, to report vandalism of a rental car. I told them kids must have done it while I was visiting. Where kids would have come from that far out in the country I didn't know, but it was their problem now, and, if nothing else, having the police check for fingerprints and the like would prevent the rental agency people from wandering out there on their own, defenceless. Not that I thought Granny would do anything, precisely. If she were going to hunt, it wouldn't be in her interest to draw attention to herself.

I was afraid of what more elaborate schemes Granny might have been planning, and it didn't help that I lacked information enough to draw any adequate conclusions. There were at least two generations of thylacines in her house, perhaps more. The sheer scale of her operation made me think she couldn't have done it all herself. Who would be mad enough to help her, and do it in absolute secrecy? It could only be someone else infected with Grief, and that, too, would be unusual. Grief attacked communities sometimes, but the Grief-stricken never worked together, not that I'd ever heard. They lacked the capacity to focus, because they were locked in on themselves and their experience of loss.

I didn't know why Granny had reached out to me. I hoped our encounter had prompted her to move more cautiously, for the sake of everyone around her. I hoped that caution would last until I discovered more of what was going on; that the potential for a too-early exposure would keep her contained long enough.

"Long enough for what, though?" George said, crammed into his window seat and stealing the last of my licorice. He'd never liked loose ends, and there were too many here for comfort. Worse, we were headed in the direction of more.

"I know it's odd," he'd said, after I'd snuffled my way to a soggy silence at yesterday's breakfast. "But I got an invitation, a couple of weeks back. Before — well." Before the Sea Witch set herself to suicide, is what he didn't say, but it was what he meant. "From an old university acquaintance. He was a friend once, but we drifted apart. I thought he was trying to reconnect. We shared a studio at one point, but he was more about design than drawing." George did biological illustrations in pen and ink. For every anniversary he'd given me a portrait of a different species of jellyfish that were almost more beautiful than the real thing. The last portrait had been of *Velella velella*, the by-the-wind sailor that made its way through the ocean entirely by chance. By necessity, *Velella* adapted to the waters it found itself in, although the wind sometimes blew it onto beaches where it stranded and died, incapable of living away from ocean.

"What was the invitation for?"

"The rebirth of a bird," he'd said. "Another resurrection. Not biological, from what I can gather. Something arty, I think, but still ..."

I'd stiffened in my seat. "That seems like too much of a coincidence."

George had smiled at me over the table, but there was no humor in it. "Doesn't it just," he'd said. His fingertips were blackened with ink, and I suspected he'd spent the flight to Tasmania sketching. He always drew when he was anxious, but he didn't show the pictures to me anymore.

"I haven't spoken to Darren in years," he'd said, and his inky fingers drummed on the table. "And I can't help but wonder if that invitation was for me, or if it was a way to get to you."

This resurrection was of a different kind. Mine had come with DNA — science and strands and the restoration of the literal dead. I was a scientist myself, and that was a rebirth that spoke to me. An event that held more art critics than scientists was uncommon ground. George was right at home. He pored over the exhibition program, explaining the rationale behind this particular resurrection. The phrase he'd used was "three-dimensional kinetic sculptures that combine biological aesthetic with socio-cultural ecological underpinnings." He could get technical sometimes, when talking about his work.

I just called them robots.

Xenicus gilviventris, the little rock wren. Poor wee beast. Endemic to the South Island of New Zealand, one of the few alpine birds of the country. Already endangered, already vulnerable to introduced predators, the rock wren had not survived the changing climate. Rats colonized the warming mountains, moving higher and higher to where they'd never been before, and the rock wren, a poor flier, could not survive the onslaught. Attempts to relocate surviving populations to offshore islands failed, and a country once known for its bird life lost yet another species.

So I learned, anyway, from the internet at airports and from George, in the air and on the way to New Zealand. He'd grown up there, in a small North Island town that existed to support regional agriculture. "Cow town," he called it, and left as soon as he could. The loss of the little bird was an old and distant thing to him, but a cause of sorrow nonetheless. "It's a grief, not the Grief," he corrected, at my expression of sympathy. "Truth is, I wasn't that attached to them. I liked the way their little eyebrows made them look so grumpy, but of all the birds we needed to save, they'd never have been at the top of my list. It's sad," he said, "but they weren't important. Weren't iconic enough, I guess."

I don't know what it was about his statement that gave me the most discomfort. The idea, still present in all its naïveté, that *iconic* was enough. The Reef had been *iconic*, and nothing had been done to stop the pale skeletal death. That iconic was a statement of worth itself, because who were we to judge which absence was the most distressing, or the least deserved? Hard to make that judgment without mirrors, but we did.

Perhaps, in the end, it was the shadow of Granny over George's face, as he spoke of a small creature who hadn't been sufficiently cared for, not by him or by anyone else. A creature that had garnered nothing but a pale admiration, enough for mild regret but not enough for Grief.

Can you watch something die and let it die?

The answer, too often, was yes.

"Except I didn't watch, did I," said George, honest to the last. "I left." So he didn't have to watch, or because he didn't care to watch?

"There's a difference? It didn't feel like my land anymore," he said. But our hotel, when we landed, was situated next to a stand of native bush, and he leaned so carefully from his bedroom window, into air that smelt of damp soil and beech trees, that I wasn't sure I believed him.

"Sometimes I think it's better not to get attached," he said. And I, so enormously attached to jellyfish, wanted to argue the point. But that was a conversation I could see quickly moving beyond the oceanic. After all, he'd let himself get attached to me, and look how that turned out. Then again, I'd been let go awfully easily. I could call it fairness and a fundamental sense of honor, that he wouldn't argue for a motherhood I did not want, but the truth was part of me wondered if he had expected to be left all along. A man who could leave himself, leave home and family and country, the ecology of his birth ... would it really surprise him that other people could leave as well? Maybe, a few years from now, he'd look back on me, on our lives together, with the same distracted fondness he felt for the rock wren. The same mild regret, only sporadically remembered. I wondered if we were both too disconnected in our own ways, or if regret was coloring my own perception, making the lines of shattering softer than they were. If marriage was attachment, then the loosening of bonds, for one who avoided attachment, could only be secret relief.

I couldn't tell anymore.

Fortunately for me, George's invitation came with a plus-one. I would have crashed the party regardless. Recent events had hardened me to social niceties. My impending divorce, the Sea Witch's brutal death ... these were bad enough without the echoes of those padded footfalls in the hallway of my memory, or the constant checking of my fingers for tooth marks that were always faint and had long since faded. I'd woken the night before the exhibit opening with bite marks from my own teeth in those same fingers, the taste of blood in my mouth. Etiquette was nothing in comparison.

"What is it these things *do*, anyway?" I hissed at George, as we politely circled the floor of Otago Museum in Dunedin, where the birds were to be presented. "Do they just, you know, hop about and stuff?" I pictured the animatronics displays in shop windows at Christmastime, the dead movements of mechanism, stiff and juddery. Something to be kept behind glass, a display piece of failed conservation not much different to the other exhibits around us, where the extinct birds of New Zealand were posed into rigidity. Dead eyes stared out of their glass display cases as if those cases were coffins.

George held a program in his hand and had clearly studied it. "These are the friendly ones. From what I understand Darren's done two sorts." He caught my querying look. "The wrens that have been programmed with realistic behavior, the ones that mimic actual rock wrens, they're the ones that'll be let loose in the mountains. These are museum pieces. They're more curious. More friendly. Designed for human interaction, and part of the exhibit is monitoring the exchange between birds and visitors to see if opinions of the wren change after interaction."

"Is that the — what was it — the 'socio-cultural ecological underpinnings'? Why doesn't he just say he's Disneyfied the thing to make it more attractive to humans?"

"He's got a grant to justify," said George. *That* was something I could understand. Artists, like scientists, always had to beg for money.

"It seems a bit late for all that, is what I'm saying." The mountains were empty of anything but rats, so getting people to love the little rock wren enough to mourn it seemed like an invitation to Grief if ever there was one. "Don't go getting attached," I said, and elbowed him gently in the side as the speeches were read, and the little robots released. My warning fell on deaf ears, because although George didn't react as loudly as the children in attendance, I'd seen fascination on his face before, the quick warming rise of wonder, and I knew what infatuation looked like on him. I'd seen it often enough in the early years of our relationship: the same tender cast to his glance, the devoted interest that took in all details. I'd been devoted too. There wasn't the smallest subtlety in that expression that I had ever missed, and nothing about it that I would fail to miss in future. Seeing him so quietly delighted by

41

something that wasn't me was surprisingly painful — it would never have hurt like this when our marriage was strong.

In all fairness, they were attractive little things. Green feathers shading into yellow and cream underneath. Their most appealing feature, as George had commented, were the slanted eyebrows that gave them permanent expressions of disgusted rage which contrasted amusingly with their flirty, fluttery movements. The bodies were round, almost tailless and with stout, widespread little legs that underlined the determined umbrage of their faces. Nothing could ever tear me away from jellies, but it was clear robotics had evolved past where my own disinterest had placed it, because these small, hopping simulacra were indistinguishable from life. If I hadn't known they were mechanism, I would never have been able to tell. Compared to the recordings of live rock wrens showing on the exhibition screens, there was no difference. The robot wrens scampered and fluttered and flew, only short flights close to the ground but flight nonetheless. They cocked their heads and flicked their wings and piped thin, high-pitched notes. The only difference from the real thing showed when someone knelt in front of them and held out a hand, palm up. The rock wren would jump into it, briefly, before bobbing back into the air and then coming back down to earth to continue their examination of the ground.

They were heavier than the real thing, but they were sweet and charming. It was hard to look at them and remember they were nothing but mirrors of the dead.

"I suppose they wind up like clockwork," I said, as George brought a bird over in his cupped hands for inspection. I reached out to stroke it — something the real bird would never have allowed — and the feathers were so soft, felt so real.

"Solar batteries," he said, almost absent in his answer. "So pretty," he said, and his voice was awe and wistfulness. "Such a pretty birdie."

I could picture him holding small animals up for a child's inspection. He'd always been good with young things, more of a nurturer than I ever was. A consequence, I thought, of the generalized wonder he'd been able to retain somehow — incomprehensible to me, who had wonder narrowed down to bells and tentacles. I couldn't understand how he could cup jellyfish, the harmless ones, in those same big hands and love them, but not love them more than anything else. It was why I had to leave him. Capacity like that should not be wasted.

"You don't trust it, do you," said Darren, as a waiter passed and we both took drinks. It wasn't a question. They were his birds, his art, but he spent more time explaining them to me than he did to George, which struck me as strange given that Darren had invited George specifically and I was merely an incidental guest.

"It's not distrust, exactly," I said, though distrust was exactly what it was. "It's more ... frustration, I guess. They weren't worth enough to save, and they're not worth enough to bring back. Not as they were, anyway."

"Disneyfied," he said, with a pained twist to his mouth. "I heard you."

"Sorry."

"No, it's true. I always thought art was meant to hurt, a little, and this does. For that reason. So I guess it's a success."

He didn't look happy, and I couldn't blame him. Debates of value and nostalgia aside, likewise the sweetening of a dead past based on a flawed assessment of worth, this was a culminating night for him, the result of many years' work, and I'd been impolite. I'd spoiled things. Trust for the new resurrectionists was thin since my encounter with Granny, only a few days since, but that was no excuse. Coincidence or not, it wouldn't do to aggravate.

"It *is* a success," I said, and gestured at the knots of people crowded around the leaping robots, completely enamoured. "I don't even like birds that much and I can see that."

"I've heard you're a jellyfish kind of girl," he said, and the smile eased his face open.

"What can I say — I like animals that have a sting to them. Perhaps it's an undiscovered artistic side of me," I said, tipping my champagne flute at him. A rock wren noticed the movement and fluttered up, perching on the rim of the glass. "It looks so *perfect*," I said, and it was unalloyed praise. Darren chuckled a little, under his breath, and it seemed like a moment to turn dispraise into tease. "It's not going to burst into song, is it?"

He laughed out loud. "I haven't gone that far, no. You'll have to go elsewhere if you want to play Snow White."

I don't know what made me say it. I hadn't made any connection — not consciously, anyway. I'd like to say it was illumination, a flash of logic and insight, but the moment after I said it, all I could think of was jellyfish and how they trailed tentacles through the water behind them, fishing for prey.

"I'm more of an Andersen girl myself. Give me 'The Little Mermaid' over the Brothers Grimm any day of the week."

"Really." That wasn't a question either, but the moment of absolute stillness in his shoulders reminded me of meat-scented breath wafting through dark corridors and the bite of small teeth on fingers. Had they been only a little older, those teeth could have drawn blood.

"Mmm. They're sadder, I think, but ultimately I find them more hopeful." This was probably the biggest lie I'd ever told in my life, as Andersen had always struck me as someone who parceled the world up into misery and portioned it out again, but I was sick of undercurrents and fishing for bait.

"I always liked the story about the Nightingale," he said. "I used to read it again and again when I was a kid. The mechanical bird that enchanted a king, and how the song of the bird — the real bird — was so beautiful that it won mercy from death."

"Don't take this the wrong way," I said, as the robotic rock wren fluttered from my glass, "but if those peeps it makes are meant to be the most beautiful song in the world, I worry for your hearing."

"The rock wren really isn't much of a singer," Darren agreed. "But it was the idea that captured me — that something so beautiful could make such a difference." He didn't say any more then, as one of the docents pulled him away to meet a donor, but I knew what he didn't say. That desire for panacea, that attempt to bargain with the inevitable. There's no nightingale alive that can turn aside the progression of Grief, once it starts, and no rock wren either. But what if there was a possibility, even so, of Grief not starting at all? How many little wrens, how many little joeys, could prevent that endless sensation of loss? Not for all, but for some.

Would it make a difference? I didn't know. It was hard to forget that the birds were mechanical. In Andersen, the simulacra broke down, and only the real bird could suffice. In this world, this much grimmer and sadder world, the simulacra, for some species, might have been all that was left.

A false resurrection, it was true. But did its deceit affect its value?

Apparently an interest in fairy tales was enough to garner a second invitation — to an area in the mountains, where the more realistic of the robotic wrens had been released. These wrens were not programed for human interaction. They were to be as natural as possible, given the information available. "I like to think," said Darren, "that people will see them when they go tramping. Just out of the corner of their eye. And it will remind them of what used to be here."

The rats might hunt these birds, but their teeth would close on metal beneath the feathers, and the robots at least would survive when their predecessors had not.

"The official release date is next month. But there's a study site, off-limits to the general public. They've been there for a few months already, so that we could observe them and adjust the programing if necessary."

We followed him to that study area two days later, and were allowed to wander while Darren checked in at a small on-site monitoring centre. "There's no guarantee you'll see one, I'm afraid," said Darren. "If I could guarantee it I'd know that I'd done something wrong." Some behavior or programing that made the bird stand out from the rocks and scrub and scree in which the wren made its home and render the camouflage of its feathers useless.

"I don't know if I want to see it or not," I said to George, as we wandered over the slopes. In some ways, absence here would be success. When I'd said as much to Darren, his expression had been all anticipation, with the barest gleam of teeth.

The mountains were alive enough, but George still shook his head when he looked at them. He could see the changes from when he was a kid, he said, a small-town boy who'd gone on school trips to the Southern Alps, to see the fading of the glaciers and the ice in a warming world. The speed of it unsettled him. It had unsettled the Sea Witch, too, when she sailed over the Reef, but that was not a comparison to dwell on.

"Do you think it's foolish," he said, "to come up here and pretend? Are we going to have a world filled with simulacra now?"

I shrugged. "Maybe pretending is better than the alternative." We'd pretended for so long, after all — that the climate wasn't changing, that the consequences wouldn't be as bad as they were. Was this really that different?

"Yes," said George, when I asked him. He peered around rocks, winced when a sudden movement turned out to be rodent instead of bird; the site was infested with them. "I'm more interested in them now than I was before." He wasn't the only one. I'd seen the reactions at the museum, how both children and adults had been charmed by a facsimile altered enough to appeal to them. I'd read the media responses, had seen the fascination there as well. The fake wrens earned far greater approval than the real ones.

It was the friendliness that did it. The fluttering and the flirting, the way the fakes made up to us. I'd like to say all I felt for the effort was contempt, but the truth was if someone had created a lion's mane jellyfish that rubbed up against me, that took my hand with friendly tentacles while we swam together, I'd have been the first in the water with it.

"Can you smell that?" said George, interrupting the fantasy.

The sweet stench of rot, of spoiling meat. And for a moment, for the tiniest microsecond, I wondered if it was dead bird we were smelling. Of course it wasn't, and couldn't be, but it just went to show how simulacra could affect even the most cynical of observers. They weren't real, but they *looked* real, and want filled in the rest. I even felt relief when I remembered that the wrens were robots and incapable of decomposition.

The smell was dead rat. At first there was only one, but the more we walked over the mountainside, the more rats we found. All of them dead, all with the smallest puncture wound in them — George noticed it first, nudging at the stiffening bodies with his boot. The punctures were often hard to see. They'd barely bled at all. Whatever it was that caused them, it was effective.

Then we saw the wren, and we knew the invitation that had come to us across oceans had not been coincidence. A robot that looked like a wren, which *acted* in all ways like a wren ... it would draw in the same predators that had killed the species, back when it was biology that fluttered over rocks, instead of aesthetic and mechanism.

"It's not possible," said George, as we watched, from a distance, as the wren flew at a rat and stabbed it, a small flash of too-small beak. The rats here were large and well-fed. "It's not enough to kill it." The rat died anyway, and quickly.

"Are you thinking poison?" I asked.

"Oh, yeah."

The wren perched on a nearby rock and watched us, too steady in its lack of movement.

"Realistic my arse," I said. "This is just as fake in its behavior as the ones at the museum." Though I had to give it to Darren: his little robots would be wonderful pest control.

"Why would he tell us these were the normal ones?" said George. He stared at the wren, suspicious. "They are *clearly* not."

"I mean, this is the study site. It's like a practice round," I said, sounding unconvincing even to myself, but before I could go any further he cut me off.

"This isn't practice. First Tasmania and now this? I said it before, Ruby. There's something dodgy going on here."

"It hasn't escaped me," I said. "Are you getting the feeling we're being shown something?"

"You're being shown something," he said, shrugging off his backpack and crouching over it, fumbling with the clasps. His eyes were still on the wren, and the wren watched us in return, the little wings neatly folded. "Here it is," he said, under his breath, pulling out the thermos by touch and unscrewing the lid, emptying coffee all over the mountainside.

"Hey!"

"I don't want to brain the thing," he said, and barely having finished his sentence, he threw the thermos, overhand with surprising accuracy. The flask landed with a dull crunch.

"I think it's pretty well brained," I said, easing over to the bird. It kicked and whirred on the rock, pathetic and broken. I tried to tell myself that it wasn't real; I felt bad for it anyway. George used the lid of the thermos to nudge the bird inside, keeping his hands well away, and capped it off.

"You better hope they don't make you pay for that," I said.

"You better hope whatever poison's pasted on that beak doesn't do for more than rats," he said.

I'd have called him suspicious, but on another island Grief had turned resurrection into something that had smacked of murder. Not directly, but I'd felt the danger all down my spine, felt the little hairs raised, and known insanity had come with teeth embedded in flesh. I'd like to say it had turned me paranoid, but we'd been lied to, here, the both of us, and birds had been used as bait.

George had been used as bait, I realized. He was never meant to go to Tasmania, and his invitation to this particular exhibit was worded to include his wife. "You should give it to me and go home," I said, meaning back to a country that wasn't his, and reached for the thermos. "Whatever this is, it doesn't have to involve you."

"Yeah, nah," said George, definitive, sliding the thermos back into his pack. "You're the scientist. Tell me, who would we see about a poison?"

"You could see me," said Darren, behind us.

4

Darren was nervous but not sorry. A certain clarity in his eyes passed for sanity, but there must have been an awareness that it wasn't a sanity we shared, because he kept himself carefully beyond arm's length. Untouchable. For the bird to enchant a king, there had to be a king to enchant, and clearly Darren thought he fit the bill. It was the monstrous obsession of Grief, taking yet another form. "It makes me see things more clearly than other people," he said. "I know you don't feel the same. Not yet."

The implication was that I would. That Grief could be induced, somehow, through outside influence, and that with it would come advocacy, or at least compliance. "I want you to understand," he said, but it wasn't understanding that I felt with extinct marsupials chewing on my fingers, and I didn't feel it here either. Recognition, perhaps, but recognizing that imbalance exists is not the same as feeling imbalance as stability.

"I just wanted to bring them back," he said.

"You haven't brought anything back," I said. "These birds ... these things you've created, they're not real. They're not alive. You know that, don't you?"

"They're beautiful," he said. As if that by itself was enough. But then, under influence of Grief, dead things often were.

"They're killing the rats," I said, and he nodded. "Can they kill anything else?"

"Just rats," he said. I didn't believe him.

"So if I were to empty the thermos and take that wren in my hands and stab you with that little beak, you'd be all right with that?"

A minor twitch, quickly covered. "Of course."

"Ruby," George interrupted, and his voice was warning-low. I waved him off.

"What if I were to stab myself?" Another twitch, this time more pronounced. "I wonder what the Sea Witch would have said about that?" It was a shot in the dark, but if what was happening in these mountains was connected to what was happening in Tasmania, then the inciting factor might have been the same. *Saner than any of us.* It was the most terrible lie.

"You're not a rat," said Darren. The words burst out of him. "Rats are ... they are ..."

"They're evil," I finished for him. "Monstrous." Some people said that about the jellies, disturbed by how the deterioration of the ecosystem was for them opportunity and blooming. And I could see — in this country of birds, where all the birds flirted with extinction, their clawed feet invitations on the path of Grief — what devouring and predators had done. "They kill everything. Indiscriminate destruction. They can't be trusted."

Monstrous. Some people said that about colonization. The coming of people like me, and what we'd done in Tasmania, the rest of Australia, and what we'd done in New Zealand ... the same devouring, the same indifference to the pre-existence of other life. The same conversation, over and over, with different settings and different subjects.

"It's so hard to stop them," he said, shoulders easing. "There are so many, and they don't care. Nothing makes them care. And when they're done they leave and go elsewhere, off the sinking ship."

"You won't get an argument from me," I said, hands spread wide to show commiseration and lack of threat. "They're better off dead."

"Yes." His expression cleared, and he was once again the man I'd met at the museum. Sane, and good-humored. It was a shock to me, having always considered Grief as linear and recognizable, how easy it was for him to cover it up. I wanted to know how far that cover went.

"Tell me something," I said, leaning forward, my voice lowering. "Is George a rat?"

I could feel George stiffen behind me – the quality of his silence was one that I had come to know well over the years. It was silence from a man profoundly uninterested in devouring, who had crossed an ocean to avoid it, but if he was being used for bait I had to know.

"I don't know," said Darren, cocking his head to one side as if he too were a wren, suspicious of interlopers. "Shall we test him?"

I didn't know what the test was supposed to be, what it was Darren thought would sway my judgment either way. There were two of us and only one of him, but insanity was not always rational, and he had poison, potentially, on his side. He also had a prior relationship with George, one that might have made him harder to hurt, but I wasn't willing to gamble my husband's safety on the remnants of friendship.

"Sounds like a waste of resources to me," I said. "If you don't remember what he was like at the museum, I do. He was as fascinated with your wrens as you are." Which was exaggeration, but it was exaggeration for purpose. What would affect Darren more than anything, I believed, was the delight George had shown at the museum, his honest fascination with the recreated wrens. That fascination, I implied, could easily turn to obsession, and from there to Grief and enlightenment. It was a measure of how badly Grief undermined intellect, I think, that my argument was accepted.

Darren gave us coordinates and sent us on our way; as little as I trusted him, residual loyalty to the woman who had been my friend made me accept the directions. He also gave us the wren — or at least had not prevented us from taking it, which was possibly more accurate. "You probably think it's proof," he said. "And it is. But it's a reminder as well. Of what the future could be."

"Just who is it you're reminding?" George asked him, eyes narrowed. If my invitation had come in the form of letters, his had been more conventional. His could also have been a proxy. We were still married, after all.

Darren smirked at him, an expression undercut by wistfulness. The desire, perhaps, to connect. "Who do you think I'm reminding? Even if you're the means to an end, your wife seems to think you can learn. I'd like to think she was right. A jellyfish should know a survivor when she sees one."

George stared at him, narrow eyed and supremely unimpressed. I knew that expression. It said "Fucking charming," or would have if he thought Darren was worth the effort of comment. Instead he said, "Come on, Ruby," and took my arm to escort me back to the car, making sure to keep his body between me and his former friend.

"The next time you are kidnapped by a crazy wolf woman, I am leaving your arse to whatever shallow grave has been assigned to you," he said, as we drove away. He always took that snippy tone, that pretense of formality, when he was upset.

I couldn't blame him. He'd put the thermos in the boot and then thought better of it. He had no doubt pictured the lid coming off as we took the twisty turns down the mountain, and he now held it between his knees, with the lid clamped down under fingers.

The resulting conversation was a familiar one.

"I'd go to the cops," said George, "but what the hell could I say? There's a mad artist up in the mountains, and his museum pieces are programmed for murder, and they fly. They only *look* like birds, so don't let them stab you with their little beaks because you might be a rat."

We shared a glance. His was colored with mechanized wings, and mine with needle-sharp teeth.

"Thing is," I said, trying to think it through, to apply logic to madness, "they're probably *not* programed for murder. At least not wholesale. Look at all the publicity around this project." There'd been photographers and journalists at the museum exhibit; it had made the evening news. "You saw how popular they were. People are going to come looking for the real ones. Well, the fakes that behave like real ones. You know what I mean. And when they find them, if they're not behaving as they should behave, someone's going to notice."

"You can't miss the rats," George agreed.

"Let's say we're not completely paranoid. Let's say the new improved rock wren can kill all sorts of intruders. The moment a family drops dead there'll be attention. The exhibit would close down and the birds would be destroyed."

"Yeah, but you're arguing like a rational person," said George. "He's not rational. He thinks he is, and granted, he couldn't have done so well putting those things together if there wasn't some reason left in him, but it's all twisted. Who's to say that one dead family isn't the point? The revenge of the rock wren is justice of a sort — the indifferent extinction of a family line, because the survivors don't care."

It made a horrible sort of sense, and I swallowed bile in order to concentrate on the driving. Typical of New Zealand, there were no barriers on the winding road, and I didn't want to steer us off the mountain. "That's ... all right, you make it sound plausible. I can't help but think he cares more about the rock wrens than what they'd kill."

"Risking a lot on that assumption, Ruby."

Risking other people, too, and that was worse. People who'd have no idea what they were walking into, but George was right. Any attempt to publicize this, or to call in law enforcement, would likely end in hospitalization for the both of us, a diagnosis of Grief that would be quickly given and then easily ignored. Even the broken bird we could hear shifting in the thermos wasn't sufficient. Not without proof of poison, and I couldn't help but think that, if it were me trying to recruit, I'd have arranged a demonstration that held only a single dose ... and neither of us had thought to bring the dead rat with us.

"Yeah. I know." The thought of that risk made me feel sick. *Can you watch something die and let it die?*

How much danger was there to other people? How much responsibility would be ours if rock wrens started picking them off? How much was Darren willing to sacrifice — how much mortality was he prepared to give his perfect little replicas? He'd worked too hard to bring them back from the dead, and was too obsessed — too enamoured — to let his replicas follow the original to extinction. I didn't think he'd let them all be destroyed. Not even for vengeance.

Grief wouldn't allow any different. It was mourning down to the marrow, the inability to let go of what had been cut away. I couldn't imagine that anyone in the grip of it would ever let go again. The roots of loss were buried too deep.

You'll have to go elsewhere if you want to play Snow White, he'd said. I'd thought it was an offhand comment, yet here in the landscape of old glaciers, I'd come across a body of water with a surface so smooth it might have been a magic mirror.

The GPS coordinates that Darren had given us led to a kettle hole. I had enough geology to recognize it as a kettle, but that was as much as I knew, so George and I scrolled through websites on our phones, looking for more information. A kettle hole was a small lake, sometimes only a pool, left behind when glaciers departed. A piece of dead ice, surrounded and buried by sediment. The resulting hole transformed into ephemeral wetlands that, in high summer, could dry out completely when precipitation levels were low.

"It's a pond," said George.

I looked at him.

"It's slightly more interesting than a pond. But I don't see why we're here, and I don't see why we should mess with it." He brandished his phone at me. "Everything I've read says they're vulnerable to disturbance. That means us."

"I'm not going to go squelching around in it!" I shot back, pre-emptively defensive. It was a small kettle, and exceedingly remote. It had taken us hours to drive to the closest road, and hours again of tramping over countryside to find. It was barely on the map — and checking the Department of Conservation website, I'd not been able to find it.

Looking back, that should have been a clue. If mirrors did nothing else, they showed us what we believed we looked like, and looking at the shimmering surface of this small body of water, fringed with turf-vegetation, tiny mosses and flowers like little white stars, I saw nothing but isolation and confusion.

"I guess I don't understand what this has to do with climate," I said, taking a muesli bar that George had ferreted out of his pack, and referring back to my phone. "In other places, warming temperatures have dried some of them up or increased temperatures in the upper levels and yeah, I can see that, but this one still looks fairly wet to me." I navigated to a paper I'd found on South Island kettles. "Though it says here changing rainfall patterns can alter the diversity of the plants within the kettle. Not that I know what the vegetation's supposed to look like."

We looked at each other blankly.

"I don't know why you're staring at me," said George. "Artist, remember? I can tell a karaka from a kōwhai, but that's about it. You're the scientist."

"I work with jellyfish. In the ocean, which is very far from here," I said. "Maybe we should, I don't know, have a closer look?"

We walked around the kettle, trying to keep as much as possible to the surrounding tussocks that grew densely about the pool. The red, thick tussocks were not easy to walk through,, their grassy strands reaching up above my waist and obscuring the ground. Keeping to the tussocks didn't give us the best view of the kettle, but any closer and we would have risked disturbing the miniature plants that fringed the water — the minute ferns and mosses and flowers that grew together in a tangled mat, and which would be more visible on the bottom of the kettle when the water dried out. Even walking as slowly as we were, trying not to miss anything, it only took a couple of minutes.

"No wonder this kettle's not on the maps," said George. "It's tiny."

"It's probably also freezing," I grumbled, wrestling my shirt over my head. There was a small break in the kettle plant turf, and it gave me the opportunity to look closer without the guilt of disturbing any more than necessary an already vulnerable site. "Don't give me that look, I'm not going to stomp along the bottom or damage anything. I'm just going to stick my head in and take a quick look. Who knows how deep it is anyway."

If I'd thought to test the water with my fingers first, we both would have got less of a shock. I inched on my belly to the edge and shoved my head under what appeared to be water — and came up immediately, shrieking, because water should have been wet and this wasn't. There was no water on my face, no water in my eyes, and my hair didn't form loose and float-ing tentacles. I scrambled back, fast, aided by George's fingers hooked in my waistband as he hovered over me.

"It rippled!" he said. "It fucking rippled!" And not like water did. I saw for myself how it appeared from a distance when he found a small rock and tossed it at what appeared to be surface. The rock disappeared, and the water wavered — unnaturally so. I crawled back to the edge of the kettle and waved my hand in that surface. It, like my head, did not come away wet.

"I think it's a hologram," I said, sitting back on my knees. "I think ... I just ..." There were no words. George didn't have any either, but he crouched next to me and waved his own hand, gingerly, in that apparent surface.

"I only brought water," he said at last, doleful. "And electrolytes. I should have brought grog. Why didn't I think to bring grog?"

"It's my fault," I said. "I had a thylacine in my lap. Then there was the poison murder-bird. I should have known we'd need wine."

"Wine, hell. I want something stronger than that."

"Oh," I said, drawing it out. "Wait till you see what's inside the damn thing."

"Spikes?" said George, in mournful tones, without the least hint of surprise. "An endless drop? A bear trap?"

"No bears in New Zealand," I reminded him. Which was unnecessary; he was the one from here, and he'd made enough cracks over the years about the comparative lack of dangerous wildlife, but the two of us were too stunned to squabble. "Lovely thoughts, by the way. No, it's worse than that."

"I honestly don't see how that's possible," said George, but he stretched out anyway, on his stomach, and I could see from the stiffness in his spine how he grimaced when his face went through that deceptive surface. Then one long arm disappeared, reaching down, and he resurfaced — if one can surface from a hologram of a pond — and his hand held a book.

Even though I couldn't see the title, I knew that book. I'd seen it before. The pages were rippled and mouldering, clumped together as if dried after long submergence, and I didn't need to pry the covers open to see the signature of the Sea Witch inside it. Marjorie, before she came to Grief, had always marked her books with a please-return-to.

"Don't say it," I said. "I know what you thought of her. Just don't say it." He'd never seen the book, but he'd heard me talk about the disintegration of Marjorie into the Sea Witch, over and over, trying to make sense of what a friend had become.

George's mouth shut with an audible click. "Right then," he said, heaving himself up with a hand squeezed on my shoulder, part of him sympathetic even if all that sympathy was for me and none for a woman he'd never much cared for. More and more, I suspected he thought her guilty of indulgence, of not fighting hard enough against loss when so many others, for so long, had endured the terrible exhaustion of greater absences. "There's got to be a power source around here somewhere, that's keeping that projection going. Why don't I go look?"

I'd not even thought of a power source. He was right: there had to be something portable, something small that blended in, that made lakes and mirrors of dry ground. The kettles were different from Reef or wrens or marsupial wolves. Vulnerable, yes, but in this part of the world they were still *there*.

I stared at the surface of the hologram. It was as beautiful as the museum wrens — finely crafted and reflective. *Mirror, mirror*, said the witch, in her search for self and the unchanging reality of her own aesthetic world. The disruption of that reality had led to temptation and murder, revulsion for the beauty of new generations. Snow White may not have been jellyfish, but if the Sea Witch could have destroyed them to bring back the beauty of the Reef, I'd no illusion that she wouldn't have done it. That, too, was Grief — the inability to balance what was left with what was left behind. Who was to say, after all, that jellyfish lacked attraction and worth, that they didn't deserve the world we'd made, the world they'd so efficiently adapted to?

I'd no illusions, either, that George's dark words couldn't reflect reality. This recreation of an ecosystem on the brink was the wrens all over again. It was opportunity wrapped up in regret, an attempt to absolve the shame of negligence and indifference by restoring as far as possible what had been lost. When I'd stuck my head under the surface, all I'd seen was a shallow depression, no more than a couple of feet deep and scoured down to bare soil where I knelt, below the only approach to the kettle that wouldn't have crushed the delicate vegetation around it. I had no doubt that the scouring was done so that the book would stand out better. The rest of the depression was filled with tussocks, and that there *were* tussocks was a late and disorienting shock — but what else would there be, in a landscape so filled with them? My fingers went through the moss and flowers and felt the same trailing fringe of red grass that covered the rest of the ground. Maybe there'd once been a small kettle here and it had dried up and gone, or been so disturbed by invasion, the influence of farming and warming temperatures, that the vegetation within had been unable to withstand the change and withered as the kettle warmed itself to extinction. But the surface of the simulation was so perfect — so blindly, blandly unthreatening — that anyone would be fooled, and anyone who chose to swim in the kettle, even to wade in it, would be vulnerable to whatever lay beneath. For all I was thinking of mirrors, beneath the reflection was a coffin as well, and its sides were made of dirt and light that shimmered like glass.

I wasn't a botanist. Kettle hole plants didn't mean much to me on an intellectual level, or even on an emotional one. But this ... this reminded me of a pitcher plant, and the bait wasn't syrup to draw me in. It was stories.

"Not just stories," said George. "Did you see what else was in there? You're the scientist," he said again. "You probably did." But I hadn't, too shocked by the absence of water, and so he showed me: took me by the hand and led me gently into the kettle. "Here," he said, pointing. I'd missed them before, so caught up in the significance of those once-sodden pages, but there were two bones half-buried, behind where the book had been. The bones were history and high school science to him, having grown up in this country. To me, an Australian whose experience of stratification tended towards currents and invisible salts, the chemoclines of lakes and ocean, beneath which were dangerous waters, unfit for jellyfish, they had less meaning.

"Look," he said, on his stomach and scraping at dirt walls. I pressed myself down flat beside him, because sitting up meant that my head came in contact with that holographic surface and it made me flinch as if it were razor-made instead of light.

"Do you think they're real?" I said.

George shrugged. "I'm more inclined toward fake," he said. "It seems a theme lately. But I wouldn't swear to it."

The larger bone was lower, and ancient. Even without George's familiarity I knew what it was, in this land of birds — a moa bone, remnant of a bird who would have towered above either of us. The upper bone was smaller, a delicate skull with a long curve of beak. "I don't know that one," I said.

"Huia," George told me. "There's no mistaking it. Not if you know even a little bit about birds here." He looked at them both for long minutes then forced them back into the wall, deliberately careless. He was usually so precise in his movements. The carelessness was a mark of contempt for whoever had put them there. If he'd believed the bones were real he'd never have handled them so roughly.

There was dirt under his fingernails. I knew he hated that. I also knew he wouldn't comment on it, so I covered his hands with my own so for a moment, at least, he wouldn't have to see. I missed what we were to each other. I knew that he missed it too, but neither of us were the type to dwell on past decisions.

That way lay misery and madness. George knew it as well as I did, and he was the first to withdraw his hands.

"Let's get out of here. This place gives me the creeps."

He wasn't the only one. "You want to tell me what that was about?" I said, climbing through the glistening surface and trying not to shudder.

"It's a reminder that we're rats," he said. "All of us." He drank from his water bottle and sighed, but reluctance had never been a reason for prevarication with him. "Look, you know New Zealand was the last major land mass to be colonized, right? And I don't mean by you lot. When my ancestors turned up here, they brought kiore with them. Rats. And hunting and hungry mouths, and so many of the birds here were flightless. They didn't have a hope. So many species went extinct. We did for the moa. Then the Europeans came and they brought more rats, different rats, and other animals too, all the introduced species together. And that was the second big wave of extinctions."

"Don't tell me. That took out the huia," I said.

"Yep. Watch it die and let it die. That's the phrase, right?" He shook his head. "I guess we all got better and better at killing. What a shock it must be, to find how efficiency in slaughter always takes the upward trajectory." He kicked dirt into the hole, watched it send the surface to shimmering. "Nasty bloody mirror," he said, under his breath, and stomped away. I let him go, let him have the time to collect himself.

Part of me wanted to toss the book in after the dirt, disturb that sinister surface, even if only briefly. Part of me wanted to chuck the wren in as well, leave bird and thermos together with the ruined book and take George, go back home, and forget this morbid tour of the resurrected dead that we'd found ourselves on, forget the bastardized creativity of pathological yearning that Grief had wrought in the world. If I threw them all in, the ripples on that holographic surface would smooth over quickly enough. If I threw them all in, eventually other ripples would smooth over too, and I'd come to forget, or at least I'd come not to dwell. I'd forget the Sea Witch, forget birds and beasts and lighted over places. Forget, too, that George had told me once, a long time ago and in passing, of people who were trying to bring back the moa as they had tried to bring back the lost tiger wolves of Tasmania. He had been trying to tell me, I think, that the world could be a home for other things than jellyfish, that we could bring children into it and there would be more for them to marvel at than tentacles. I think he thought I'd forgotten that.

I could forget it all now. I could. I'd make sure of it.

"Ruby." George beckoned me over, disturbance now smoothed so well I'd not have known it was there if I hadn't experienced it with him. "Take a look at this." He led me around the kettle, demonstrating, using an artist's eye to uncover artificiality. "This is really an amazing set-up. I'd admire it if I wasn't so damn revolted."

"Is it bad I'm wondering what someone could bury in a place like this? Something other than bones, I mean."

"I wondered it first," he said. There was a long silence, in which he carefully did not look at me. "I know you don't want to talk about her." He held up his hands. "I'm not saying this to be difficult. But that book, and this place, and this weird-arse trip that's centered on you and this twisted version of restoration of animal and place, don't you think ... I mean, have you wondered whether or not your witch friend is actually fucking dead?"

Of course I'd wondered. I'd wondered since the moment I understood, head under that apparently watery surface and staring at dry earth, that what I'd seen, that what I thought existed, had been pure construction.

"I saw her die."

Can you watch something die and let it die?

"I *let* her die," I told him. I'd never told anyone before. "I pulled myself out of that pool and I looked back at her and the real jellyfish were pouring in, mixing with those horrid plastic simulacra she'd made, and the water was rising and rising, and all the blood from where her tongue had been, and I could have run to her, round the edge. I could have reached out to her, encouraged her to swim to the side. If she had I might have been able to pull her out. Even if she'd been stung, even if she'd been stung a lot, first aid and a hospital might have saved her.

"I didn't even *try*," I told him. The Grief had had her so long, and it had been so hard to watch, and then it had been over. I told myself that I'd saved her future pain, for she would have tried again — they all did. While this was the truth, it was not all of it. "I saw her die," I said again, but if the past week had shown me anything, it was that death, even extinction, was both too much and not enough.

5

The flight back to Australia was quiet. The wren, still in its thermos, was buried in a suitcase, stuffed round with clothes. It hadn't stopped shuffling so I'd killed the power, and when still it looked enough like a sculpture to pass for artwork. "It hasn't seen sunlight for days," George had grumbled when I disconnected the solar battery using tweezers from my make-up kit. "When's the stupid robot going to die?" He'd insisted we take the first flight we could. I hadn't even had time to shower.

I had more to concern myself with than hygiene, or solar batteries. The Andersen was in the overhead locker. I wanted to take it out, hold it on my lap and trace the swollen pages with my fingertips. Although tactile sensation sometimes aided understanding, I didn't believe that this time it would have helped. The book was a symbol, that was all — not even a universal one. Fully half the stories I'd propped myself up with since I'd left home were found in the pages of other story books entirely, for all fairy tales were a linking theme. What had been left beneath that holographic kettle hole wasn't any kind of road map. It was a calling card, the leavings of a woman I'd known, once, who had turned into someone fundamentally unknowable. For so long, I'd told myself that Grief was an aspect of personality instead of all of it, thinking that the vestiges of Marjorie that I'd seen surface and sink in the sustained mourning of the Sea Witch's mind meant that she was still there, at least in part. That was always the hardest part of Grief — the realization that the absence, and the loss, was total.

The Marjorie I knew had been playful, but games like this weren't for her. They were too cruel in their ambiguities. And now I had to face the fact that the Sea Witch might exist, still, using the body of my friend as a conduit. It was a little too much like resurrection, again — the raising of the dead for purpose, because the loss of those dead was too great.

If the Sea Witch did exist, it meant that the scene at the pool had been nothing but farce. For what purpose, I didn't know, but the farce would have been extensive. Holographic, perhaps? With the water real, and the appearance of jellies rising up beneath me, so that I was never in it with them, so that I never broke through the layers of pretence to see it for what it was. If so, it required more engineering knowledge than Marjorie had ever possessed. It also required a certainty on the Sea Witch's part that I would let her go, and that my actions would not interfere enough to break the illusion. It required that others not break it as well. The rising body count of Grief had led to less investigation by doctors — a diagnosis was thought to be enough, and rarely did any medical examiner require an autopsy of those whose suicide came from Grief. Even so, I'd called emergency services, and they'd come, and the body had been extricated and examined, prepared for funeral. It had been buried. I'd attended the service. For all those things to come to pass, the Sea Witch would have to be dead.

Or she'd have to be treated as dead, by those who knew enough — who had privilege and access enough — to cover for her, to make the appearance of her passing solid and undeniable.

If that were true, Grief had spread further than I had ever guessed. Worse, those who helped her had passed — were passing — as unaffected. Tasmania had taught me that was possible. Granny had been able to retain an appearance of trustworthiness long enough to exploit the research project she was involved in, and to destroy what she no longer needed when she left it. Darren, smiling for photographers and celebrated by the public for his restoration of the rock wren, had managed to deceive everyone around him when he'd reprogramed the wren and released it on the mountainside. And I had no idea who was recreating kettle holes in landscapes, but clearly they had access to sophisticated technology or they wouldn't have been able to simulate the kettle in the first place. There was no way to predict how they'd use those resources in the future.

It was the ambiguity of it all that disturbed me the most. I'd seen at the museum how willing people were to be enraptured by the return of the dead. I'd felt the fascination myself, in Tasmania. It was the reason George and I were both still reluctant to contact authorities. Even if they did show up, suspicious of Grief in us if not in others, there were such easy explanations, and no evidence we had amounted to any sort of proof that the recreations we'd seen were hostile. For most, our recent encounters with the resurrected dead were something to be celebrated. Even if the wren we'd taken was found to have poison seeping from it, all Darren had to say was that the poison was meant for rats. He'd probably be feted for it.

The only path forward was to do nothing. I'd like to say it was a decision that came hard, but the truth was a life spent glorying in the now-abundant jellyfish was good practice for looking away. The things I loved survived climate change. They flourished in it. That other species did not was regrettable, but not undermining. I'd managed to distance myself from loss.

The divorce was my doing, or so I told myself. True, the differences were irreconcilable, but we might have staggered on longer, content if not actually happy. I'd seen the coming schism and anticipated, pushing away because I could, and because it was easier to take the loss than to fight against it.

So many things came easily to me. I'd become inured to loss. And now, when I didn't know what to do, I fell back into easy. George dropped me off at my apartment, and handed over the thermos without argument. Neither of us wanted it. I kicked it under the bed and left it there, put the battery in my bedside drawer because I didn't want to reconnect it and reanimate the wren. The constant shuffling would have kept me awake. It would have kept me *aware*. With the silence, some days I didn't even remember the thermos and its dead contents until I was on my third cup of coffee. Even then it was a minor mental effort to forget it again. George didn't remind me. I didn't hear from him, and refused to consider what that might mean, or who he might have been talking to instead.

Minor as it was, that forgetful effort collapsed in on itself when the Sea Witch sauntered into my office, and settled herself in the chair across from my desk. It was the chair students sat in when they came to query the syllabus; it didn't take me long to realize that I was the one who should be sitting in it.

"I wish I could say your reaction was a surprise," said the Sea Witch. "I was hoping for better." Her skirt was still ragged. Plastic was twisted round her arms, in the braids of her hair, but what struck me most was that she was capable of speech. The last time I'd seen her, she'd cut out her own tongue ... yet the woman I saw before me had that tongue firmly rooted inside her mouth.

"It was too much," said the Sea Witch, after I gaped and stammered through greeting. "I needed to think. I needed to *work through* thinking. It wasn't as if speech had done much for me back when I was alive."

There was too much to work through. The memory of journals under my fingers, yes, the failed warnings of environmental advocacy. It hadn't been enough, and I couldn't say I was entirely surprised she'd come to resent the work that hadn't been enough to keep coral alive. I resented it sometimes too — the repeated arguments that changed so few minds and fewer practices. The endless pained exhaustion of a fight we were never going to win. That small shared sympathy was drowned, though, by the horror and mystery of her presence.

"When you were alive?" I repeated, inelegantly. "You're not bloody dead." That at least I was sure of. The Sea Witch sat before me and she wasn't a robot, or a hologram, or grown in a lab. She was a living being that hadn't died yet.

"No?" she said. "Watch this." She'd left the door open, and one of our colleagues walked past. His nose, as always, was buried in a book. "Hi, Sandy!" said the Sea Witch.

He looked up and smiled, and then something happened to that smile. It froze, just slightly — an expression I'd seen on him before, at faculty fundraisers, when he was talking to someone he should have known but couldn't place. "Hey!" he said. "Great to see you. Sorry I can't stop to chat. Gotta run."

"Told you," said the Sea Witch. "People hear you've got Grief and they stop looking. Afraid to see their own futures, I expect."

"I didn't stop looking." The opposite, in fact. I'd kept on looking, kept on visiting, bringing paper and plastic and the remembrance of a friendship that I wasn't sure I wanted anymore. A friendship that became more burdensome by the day.

"You keep telling yourself that," said the Sea Witch.

"You think I'm lying?"

"I did appreciate it. The effort. The attempt at empathy. Though let's not pretend your devotion was the result of anything but a determination to retain a certain level of self-respect in the face of imminent deprivation. You were losing a friend, and good people don't abandon their friends, or not easily, so you stayed until I gave you the proper opportunity to let go." She poked her tongue out at me and waggled it, playful. "But good people don't let go either — not the way you did — so when the chance came again, when a packet of letters arrived in your mailbox ... Tell me, was it a chance to paper over what you'd done?"

I sat back in my chair, and kept my gaze locked on hers because the alternative was worse. "Can you watch something die and let it die? Yeah, I got the message, thanks. I could, and I did, and I honestly don't know how to feel about that. If you give me a few more months I'll learn to live with it. In a year or two I probably won't even feel bad."

The Sea Witch grinned, and it was honest admiration. "I've always liked that about you," she said. "Monstrous self-interest masquerading as emotional stability."

"Not all of us feel the need to beat our breasts so damn publicly."

"Resentment, much?"

There was nothing to say to that. Partly because it was true, and mostly because it was awful. For all I'd tried to cling to Marjorie after she'd begun her transformation into the Sea Witch, it was a clinging that came with condescension. Grief had made such a wasteland of society. It was constant reproach — that we hadn't done enough, and that we weren't sensitive enough. No one ever wanted mental illness, but deep inside there remained the wondering: why hadn't I succumbed? What was lacking in me that I could see the world change so profoundly, and with such loss, and do nothing but shrug? Oh, not in my actions. I researched. I was an advocate for biodiversity and climate mitigation. Many of the absences did hurt. Yet those hurts were brief, and I got on. And part of me, the small secret part that I didn't like very much, looked down on those who couldn't.

"Say it," said the Sea Witch.

I said nothing.

"*Say it.*"

"I wish you'd stayed dead," I said, finally. "Life was easier when you were dead. I didn't have to try and fight for you anymore. I didn't have to pretend it was possible to fight for you." I wondered, briefly, if this was how George felt. If this was the reason he left the home he was born in. The reason he hadn't tried harder to make me stay in the home we'd made together.

"And now you can't pretend you have to think," mocked the Sea Witch. Her mouth was a small, mean moue, and she reached for one of the licorice pieces I kept in a bowl on my desk, her tongue twining about it. "And choose. How's George, by the way?" Her smirk told me she already knew, but I answered anyway.

"Fine. We signed the divorce papers this morning." Afterwards I'd driven him to the airport, slipped licorice into his pocket, and waved goodbye as he flew back to New Zealand. I hoped it was to visit his family. I hoped it so hard I didn't ask for confirmation. It was no longer my business.

"No distractions, then."

"Not for you." This was a conversation we'd both been waiting for. Even not knowing if she was still alive, and not knowing if she'd show up if she were, I'd still been waiting for it.

"Or for him," she said. "I wonder what he's open to doing now, your no-longer husband?" She smiled again. "All the pieces of your old life, just washed away. All the structure gone out of it. All the structure that meant something anyway. Home. Work. You've not gone near a jellyfish since you got back from New Zealand. Not written a single word about them."

"You've been watching me." Of course she had. For all her disgust with medusae, I'd begun to see that the Sea Witch had tentacles in everything. I shouldn't have found it surprising. All organisms found their niche eventually.

"I've seen what happens when structure fades away," she said. "When the skeleton bleaches white and all the coral dies. Something needs to take its place."

"What is it you're trying to build?" I asked the Sea Witch. *The sanest of them all*, Granny had called her, but this wasn't sanity. It was opportunism. It was adaptation to environment — the jellyfish way, to flourish in a warmer ocean. Perhaps to survive in this new world that climate had made, opportunism, for some, was the clearest path to sanity.

"I don't want to build anything," said the Sea Witch. "I want the old world back."

"It's not coming back. We killed it. We watched it die and we let it die. Isn't that what you've been telling me all along?"

The Sea Witch waved a hand, indifferent. "You knew that. I gave you motivation to admit it. I'm more interested in aftermaths. Have you never wondered? The proficiency we showed. The indifference. When we saw how good we were at killing, when we made it part of us. Did you think it would just go away?"

I didn't think of it at all. But now that I did, the inevitability was plain.

"All the creatures that died when the Reef did. The venomous, the camouflaged, the predators. All those empty spaces. What did we expect to fill them with, if not ourselves?"

That was the genesis of Grief, laid open. Come not from what we'd done to the other, but what we'd done to ourselves. No wonder it all ended in suicide. Self-knowledge was the clearest thing in the world. It was also the unkindest.

"At least it never left me voiceless," said the Sea Witch, when I told her so. "I looked into a mirror, and saw something die, and I *let* her die, because she had to. She'd earned it. That's what I told her. And when I let her go, that woman in the mirror, all that was left was knowledge. I could watch something die and let it die, and I could do it over and over.

"Suicide," she said, leaning over my desk, her breath smelling of salt, "is not the only way."

Grief ended in death, always. "You want me to take up murder."

"I want you to be what you are," said the Sea Witch. "Someone who loved the glory and wonder of the world." *Golden jellyfish, migrating through lake water.* "Someone who loves it still." *Not looking down to the layers beneath, the dark waters, and dangerous.* "Grief was never about the loss. It was about the killing, the sheer culpable *scale* of it. You're selfish enough to survive the knowledge, that's all. And once you know what you are," she said, "you know what you can do."

No more sharks in the Reef. No more sea snakes, no more stonefish. Just the things that killed them.

"Don't you want to pay them back?" said the Sea Witch.

I wondered how many of them there were. How many had taken their Grief and forged it into weaponry, made marvels come from anger and given their hearts to the dead instead of the living. How many could no longer look in the mirror, knowing what they had done, and how they had thereby impoverished both the world around them and themselves.

"When I go out to the Reef now, it's all dead but for the jellyfish," said the Sea Witch.

I loved jellyfish. I did. Sometimes, with George gone, they felt like the only things I loved.

"It's so lonely there," mourned the Sea Witch.

I would not cry. I wouldn't.

Acknowledgments

This novella was written in the first half of 2020, during my time as a visiting artist at Massey University and the Square Edge Arts Centre in Palmerston North, Aotearoa New Zealand. It was my first writing residency, although not my last, and is likely to remain the strangest. Only a few days after I arrived, the country went into strict lockdown in order to tackle the global COVID-19 pandemic. I was confined to the Square Edge flat for weeks. The building was deserted. The entire city center was deserted. The university was closed. Everyone stayed home. I went to the supermarket once a week, masked and socially distanced. Everything else was rigid isolation. I read articles about how people in lockdown were missing animals; how nature cams like the one focused on albatross down in Taiaroa Head, Dunedin, were suddenly experiencing a massive upswing in views. We were ecologically deprived and desperate to connect. Not so surprising, then, that a story of reaction to ecosystem loss came out of a residency defined by absence.

Thanks are due to the staff of the School of English and Media Studies at Massey, who did their best to make me feel part of the academic community even though I never met most of them in person, and was never able to visit the office they had arranged for me on campus. Thanks are also due to the staff of Square Edge, who were enormously kind and supportive. Particular thanks should go to Laura Jean McKay and Thom Conroy from Massey, and Karen Seccombe from Square Edge, who took with good grace my daily emails full of increasingly revolting animal facts, proof that I was still there, still working, and at least relatively sane under very trying circumstances. I am enormously grateful for their support.

About the Author

Octavia Cade is a New Zealand writer. She has a Masters in biology and a PhD in science communication, and she likes using speculative fiction to talk about science in new and interesting ways. She's primarily concerned with climate fiction — her climate novel, *The Stone Wētā*, was published in 2020 by Paper Road Press — and how humans might cope with the challenging world that climate change will bring. She's sold over 50 stories to markets such as *Clarkesworld*, *Asimov's*, and *Strange Horizons*. Two poetry collections, a short story collection, an essay collection on food and horror, and several novellas have been published by various small presses. She has won three Sir Julius Vogel awards for speculative writing, and is an HWA and SFWA member and Bram Stoker nominee. Octavia attended Clarion West 2016, and was a 2020 visiting artist at Massey University/Square Edge in NZ.

She would totally bring back the moa if she could.

STELLIFORM PRESS

Earth-focused fiction. Stellar stories.
Stelliform.press.

Stelliform Press is shaping conversations about
nature and our place within it. Check out our
upcoming titles and articles and leave a comment or
review on your favourite social media platform.

9 781777 091767